CASTAWAY WIFE

A SURVIVAL GAME OF PASSION

KENNY WRIGHT

WORDS

A Word on the Inspiration

I've been a fan of the CBS show, *Survivor*, for many years. This is coming from someone who resisted watching reality television initially, and to be honest, am still not a huge fan of the genre. I don't watch *Real Housewives* or *The Bachelor* (but don't judge anyone who enjoys those!). A friend turned me on to *The Amazing Race*, which I still love (although this last season was a bit meh), and when he introduced me to *Survivor,* I was hooked. There is something about the community that forms every season, the love-hate relationships between the cast, mixed with the physical challenges, the twists, and all the drama, that I just love. I've wanted to write an erotica version of it, but it's hard to get sexy when everyone is dirty and tired, without stretching the, um, reality too much.

Then I realized something. What if we write this not from a contestant on a show like that, but from the *husband's* perspective, who's sitting at home having to deal with his wife on an island with a bunch of hot, undressed men? Extending that, what if the actual book dealt with the aftermath of the show, not the show itself. And thus, *Castaway Wife* was born.

A Word on the Process

What you're holding is the final product of a book that's gone through more than a few iterations and revisions—like all good pieces of fiction and *literally everything that I write*. This one, unlike any other book, was initially published entirely on Patreon. It was a bit of an experiment, because this thing wasn't designed to be read as a serial, and the version you're now holding in your hands is not exactly the same thing that was published there.

I do think the process was pretty cool, though, so I'll write a few things here. When I started to post, my draft at the time was pretty chaotic. The sequence of events jumped all over the place, as it was designed to be a series of flashbacks told from events at the end of the book. That proved to be too confusing to follow, so as I started to publish the chapters online, I was constantly reworking the sequence. This, in turn, helped me see things in new ways, which changed scenes that I hadn't yet posted. The constant and regular feedback from so many "beta readers" was also amazing.

Finally, only about half of this book was done when I started to post it on Patreon. I added some new scenes at the end, of course, but a lot of the new content came from scenes that I beefed up in the middle in support of the story as a whole. It was a truly live writing experience. Pretty cool. Also, a lot of work and kind of stressful at times to make deadlines, but in the end, so worth it.

So much so, in fact, that I did it again on an even lengthier series called *In Too Deep* (head over to Patreon if you're interested in that).

1

AND THE WINNER IS...

"And the winner of Season 25 of Castaway is..." Molly Reynolds, long-time host of the hit reality game show, Castaway, paused for dramatic effect, studying the three finalists. They were holding each other's hands, supporting one another despite the weeks of fierce competition.

Molly turned her television smile outward, where the live audience was seated, silent, tense, anticipating the announcement. Her smile radiated even farther, picked up by the cameras and broadcast around the world. At home, everyone held their breath as Molly Reynolds delivered the news.

"The winner is Jason. Congratulations, Jason."

The audience rose to their feet, starting to cheer. The camera operators zoomed in on Jason, the newest winner of the show, as the two other finalists pretended to be happy for him, congratulating him. The rest of the contestants, whose votes had crowned Jason the winner, swarmed in around the three in a happy reunion as Molly Reynolds stepped out of the fray.

"We're going to a commercial break," she announced to the camera right in front of her. "But we'll be back to catch up with Jason, as well as some of our favorite moments. Did Clay really enjoy eating those grubs? How does Janice feel about being seen as the mom of the group? And we definitely want to talk about all the showmancing that went on this season. Was any of it real? All coming up right after the break."

She stopped talking as the camera lights went dark, but the celebration on stage went on. The emotions were real. For the group up there, they'd spent an intense month together on a deserted island, sweating, competing, fighting, and bonding. This live show wasn't just about finally learning who won the whole competition, but it was a family reunion. Everyone in the audience, even those who were literally family, could only stand and watch like outsiders.

That's certainly how Andy felt, clapping from his seat in the audience as his wife, Chelsea, hopped around the stage with her Castaway family. He didn't know them any more than the rest of the viewing audience, who'd watched the same twelve episodes that he had. But he knew Chelsea, and she was happy, and he was happy for her.

He also knew that somewhere, there could be a camera on *him* now, and he wasn't going to show the world his cuckold angst.

Chelsea turned from her reunion and found Andy in the crowd, her brows knitted ever so slightly. He smiled at her and nodded. When she returned it, her beauty took his breath away. Enhanced by the makeup, the hair, the shaped eyebrows and all the other styling the network had done to get her TV ready, she barely looked like the girl he'd met so long ago.

Andy and Chelsea always loved these live episodes of Castaway. They'd watch them from the sofa in their home, amazed at how different the contestants looked a full three months after their return home. On the show, they slept under the stars without access to showers or soap or hair brushes or makeup. Months later, the dirt and grime of the island long washed away, it was like they were different people, glamorous versions of their more real selves.

Andy was now having that sensation with his own wife. The dress the network stylist had chosen for her was tighter and shorter than anything she'd normally wear, pale pink with a scooping top that did more than just hint at her cleavage. They'd straightened her soft, caramel brown hair, which fell freely around her shoulders—so different from the tight braid she wore for most of the show. She was a vixen—normally his vixen, but right now, he knew the social media circles were blowing up about how the buxom Chelsea, the hottie librarian, looked in the show.

Chelsea locked eyes with Andy, about to step down and join him there in the audience when someone from the studio stopped her, whispering into her ear and directing her back to the stage. The commercial break was almost over. Time to go into the post-show.

She blew a kiss and let herself be directed up onto the risers with the rest of the cast, smiling and nodding to her new friends.

More than the hair, the makeup, or even the dress, it was Chelsea's confidence that struck Andy as the biggest change. She didn't shy away from the lights or the makeover. She didn't seem to want to recede back into her shell as she gave hugs to people who'd been strangers just a few months ago. She wore her confidence as naturally as she wore that dress.

***

WHEN THE LIVE show came back from commercial break, Molly Reynolds was perched before the assembled contestants, now basking beneath the bright, studio lights.

"We had a few showmances this season," she said with a laugh. Turning to the cameras, she added, "Even I got caught up in the rumor mill, and let me say to you all, while I'm flattered, there's nothing there."

Castaway used the same structure that many successful reality TV shows used. There was about an hour of edited drama as the cast hung out on the beach, bonding, conniving, and competing against one another. Then, at the end of each episode, all of the remaining players in the game would come together to vote someone off of the show, as those who'd already been voted off watched.

Prior to this vote, though, Molly Reynolds would gather everyone and discuss what went down in the episode. This is where she really shined, able to tease out juicy drama and keep everyone's paranoia up.

Those who were cast away formed the group of people who would eventually vote on the winner of the show, so it was almost as important not to upset their opponents as it was to outmaneuver them.

Jason, the just-announced winner of Season 25, did this by being the lovable flirt, and it worked. It was a running joke. Somehow, through raw charisma, he pulled it off without being a creep. No woman was spared his flirty banter. Not even Molly Reynolds.

See, besides being a very experienced and capable host, Molly was a total knockout. Half-Korean, half-American, she'd done modeling in her twenties. Now, in her mid-40s, she was even more stunning. Jason engaged with that side of her more than any contestant in the last 24 seasons, and audiences noticed how it made Molly blush. The unflappable was flapped.

Andy had asked Chelsea about it as they watched the episodes together with the rest of the television world. "Was there something there?"

"Jason and Molly? I... don't know." Chelsea had seemed weird about it at the time, but she'd not been very forthcoming about anything at the time. Andy had chalked it up to her worrying about violating her NDA.

Jason had also flirted with Chelsea early on, but their alliances diverged, so it didn't go anywhere. Still, despite those alliances, she liked him enough that she cast her vote for him in the end and helped him win.

The Castaway host brought Andy back into the moment. "But we're not talking about me," she said, turning back to the assembled contestants. "First, Brooklyn and Kyle, the question everyone wants to know... are you still together?"

Andy zoned out again as the two contestants, who had a very visible on-air "showmance", announced that they were now engaged.

Instead, Andy's focus was on Chelsea, sitting up there, listening to Brooklyn and Kyle rehash their spark. He also watched Todd, sitting in a seat two spots away. The two were not looking at one another, but that lack of eye-contact felt so deliberate

Andy shifted in his seat as that familiar, itchy discomfort rose through him. He'd felt it every time he thought about all the guys who'd hit on Chelsea over the years. He'd felt it strongly watching the show, seeing her and Todd, reading the forum discussions long after Chelsea had gone to bed.

Molly Reynolds again. "Brooklyn and Kyle weren't our only showmances. We had a few others brewing, like this was a season of Love Island. How about it, Chelsea? Tell us it wasn't all part of the game."

The subject had finally turned to Chelsea, who maintained her poise, hands in her lap, smile almost innocent in nature. "Well, I think that when you share such an intense experience with a small group of people, it's only natural that they develop a connection."

Andy felt clammy, achy. He quickly wiped sweat from his

brow. Andy noticed as his insides twisted that Todd was watching Chelsea just as intensely.

Molly Reynolds didn't let Chelsea off the hook so easily. "So your 'connection' with Todd was real."

At last, she looked across at the man in question, a brawny fireman from LA, covered in tattoos and still sporting a more trimmed version of the scruff he'd grown over the course of the show. Andy—and the rest of the watching audience—leaned in for this answer. Chelsea said, "A partnership or alliance or whatever doesn't need to be a 'showmance,' Molly."

"Sure." Molly nodded, looking amused. "How about it, Todd?"

"I mean, I think we had a good... partnership. But then again, I also got totally backstabbed by her. Didn't see that vote coming."

It was a huge play on Chelsea's part. They were down to just five players. Chelsea and Todd were in a strong alliance and had a great chance to make it to the final two. Then, Chelsea switched sides and cast the pivotal vote to cast Todd away. It was a strong enough play that it spooked the remaining three, who voted her off the next week.

"Those hard feelings, Todd?" Molly probed.

Todd shrugged. "It's a game. I probably should have done it myself, but she had me totally fooled." He chuckled. "We worked it out, though, in the end. No hard feelings, Chels."

Chels. The familiarity between these two was palpable. America had watched it build each week as they formed their strong alliance. Andy didn't see his wife anymore, but the Castaway character that they'd edited and crafted.

It was the character that he'd clung to with each episode. It had been fun at first, then it got uncomfortable as she grew closer to Todd. Andy told himself it was the editing. He told himself that it was okay to be turned on by their flirtation. He told himself that it was just a fantasy.

"Let's turn to David and Harry," Molly said, shifting the spotlight away from Chelsea and Todd. "Was your showmance real?"

Andy zoned out again. He was staring at Todd and Chelsea, who were still holding eye-contact, as Todd's final words reverberated in his head, making him so queasy, and so hard.

We worked it out...

In the end...

But first, we go to the beginning.

2

GETTING READY

Five and a half-months before that live show, and only three days before Chelsea was to get on a plane, heading for the Caribbean, Chelsea stood before the mirror in a bikini and frowned at herself.

"I can't... wear this," she said.

"You can," Andy encouraged. "You look great."

She did. The pale pink halter bikini wasn't all that risqué, as bikinis go, but on her tall body with her generous curves, she could have fit right at home on the cover of *Sports Illustrated*.

"It'll fall off when I'm doing a challenge," she said.

"I don't think it will." Andy moved up behind her, admiring her reflection. It was a sturdy bikini—no loopy bows that could snag on things, no part of it was banded in flimsy string. The bottoms fully covered her heart-shaped ass, and the top held her full tits in place.

But it was a *bikini* that Chelsea would wear on national television. It was a lot of skin to expose. If things were reversed, Andy didn't think he'd be able to wear something so revealing. Then again, he didn't have a va-va-voom body like Chelsea,

who'd been working out hard over these last few months, tightening and toning and training to be on Castaway.

"You look great," he whispered behind her. He touched her
skin at her hip, warm and silky smooth, tracing it up and around
her body. She'd always been healthy, but now she had tone—flat
stomach, shapely back and arms, muscular, shapely thighs.

Chelsea looked better than great, and it was giving Andy a
hardon. He pressed it against her from behind. She stopped her
scrutiny of herself and found his eyes in the mirror. It was still
difficult getting used to seeing her without the glasses that he'd
always known her with. She'd gotten LASIK for the show, too,
joking that she'd be kicked out of the librarian society for it.

"I'm going to miss you," she said. "I don't know that I can do
any of this."

"You can." Andy squeezed her from behind. "You're going to
go out there and win us a million dollars."

Castaway followed the familiar formula for reality shows
that came out of the early 2000s. A group of strangers were put
on an island together with very few provisions. They competed
for tools and food and the right to remain on the island. Every
few days, they had to "cast" one member "away," with a secret,
group vote. There was a lot of maneuvering, alliance forming,
and backstabbing. Made for great TV.

Chelsea introduced it to Andy when they were first dating,
and she vowed to be on it one day. He still couldn't believe that
his sweet, quiet wife would want to be on such a cutthroat game.
She never sought out exposure or attention, but there was something about *this* particular game that drew her. He loved that
about her.

She turned in his arms. Despite being 5' 9", she had to look
up at Andy to meet his eyes. He was still convinced that his
height was one of the only reasons she settled for him. For she

most certainly settled. He was definitely hitting above his league.

She had large, expressive, dark eyes that the American audiences were going to love, with a smattering of freckles across her cheeks and skin that already glowed with a golden tan. She'd been conditioning that, too, not wanting to burn while on the island.

"You've been training for this moment." He brushed a thumb along her cheek. "You'll never forgive yourself if you back out now."

She nodded. He was right, and she knew it. She'd have all the regrets if she didn't go, even if she was the first to be voted off.

"But what I *can* give you is something to look forward to, once you're back home." He leaned in and kissed her softly. He reached behind her, filling his hands with her butt—a butt she always complained was too big despite all of Andy's reassurances. "You're so sexy, Chels."

He kissed her again, pushing his tongue past her lips. She relaxed into the embrace, her hands moving into his hair as she pressed her body against his. They turned, moving towards the bed as he reached behind her neck and unfastened her bikini top.

They rolled onto the sheets, Chelsea's dark hair spilling over the pillows. Andy climbed over her, planting a knee between her thighs as they kissed again. He could feel the heat and the need build in her. He wanted her to remember this moment, and how good he could make her feel.

"Mmm, yes," she sighed as he moved his attention to her tits. She had juicy, coral nipples that swelled up when she was excited. They were swollen now, puckered into thick eraser tips that Andy swirled with his tongue, just the way she liked it.

But as much as he loved her breasts, he was on a mission to

truly blow her mind. He sank down between her legs, kissing along her stomach. He could feel her abs flexing beneath his lips, the buzzing energy of anticipation. Her breath caught as he grasped the sides of her bikini bottoms and tugged.

To prepare for spending up to a month on an island without any provisions or niceties, Chelsea had her teeth whitened and her hair laser-removed nearly everywhere but on her head. For Andy, that preparation alone made the whole experience worth it.

"Your skin is so soft," Andy said as he traced his hand up the outside of her thigh. While he reveled at the skin beneath his fingers, his eyes were locked on her sex, now completely bare. He was still surprised that she'd opted to remove all of it, but Chelsea didn't do things halfway.

He could smell her excitement, see it moisten her mound. He dove in, unable to resist her any longer, his tongue flicking along her exposed clit.

"Ngh!" she cried, stiffening as his mouth touched down. "Yes!"

They'd been all over one another in the lead up to the show. It was like rediscovering his wife all over again, which he could still remember so vividly. She'd been nerdy when they'd met in college, hiding her body in baggy clothing and her beauty behind her thick, shaggy hair. He thought she was pretty, but attainable. It was only after they hooked up that he realized how out of his league she was.

Chelsea still saw herself as that nerdy girl from college. The national audience wouldn't, and Andy knew it. He knew that on the other side of the show, a new world would open to his wife. She'd no longer see herself as the mousy academic. With her hourglass figure and covergirl face, coupled with her approach-able personality, she'd be a sex symbol.

Andy lapped at pussy, working her clit until his tongue

ached. She always loved it when he ate her, and Andy wanted her to remember this orgasm when she was alone and missing home...

Or when she was hanging out on a remote beach with other, equally attractive participants in nothing but her underwear. National audiences wouldn't be the only ones to notice what she always tried to downplay.

"Oh, Andy!" she gasped.

He worked her faster, pressing two fingers into her smooth sex. Would someone else discover the lack of a bush? Lonely and horny, would Chelsea cuddle up beside another man for warmth at night, only for it to lead to more?

The questions were like a whip cracking behind him. He ate her to a loud orgasm as he fought back his own premature one. The insecurities were back. They'd been with him since that first hookup. They were there when he'd watched her walk down the aisle in a white dress that didn't even attempt to hide her beauty. They'd been there every day of their marriage. When would she find someone else? When would she realize that she could have anyone?

"Andy! Andy, too—ahh! Too much!" She was pushing him away, her body going too sensitive, ravaged by her loud orgasm. Andy hadn't heard it, so focused on what was to come.

"Sorry, sorry," he gasped, pulling his head out from between her thighs. He couldn't resist one last lap across her mound, though, just to feel all that silky skin where she'd always kept a trimmed bush. That part of her was now gone forever.

He climbed up over her, his kisses drawing shudders on her sensitive skin. Once again, he feasted on her nipples, kneading her soft, natural breasts, pressing them together.

Chelsea tugged at his shirt, wanting to feel his skin on hers. She pulled him in for a kiss on the mouth as they kicked off his pants and freed his cock. Silently, she guided him to her pussy, gliding the tip along all that soft skin before taking it inside of her.

Chelsea and Andy made love. It was comfortable and familiar, like snuggling into a warm bed, or sipping creamy coffee in the morning. They knew what each liked, teasing out the pleasure in the gentle rise and fall of their hips.

But for Andy, there was an edge that night, a desperate need to prove himself to her. This was what she had to come home to. He was her comfort. He was her constant. No matter what happened. No matter how much the show would change her.

Andy started on top, but ended on the bottom, with Chelsea rising over him, riding his cock, her voluptuous body bouncing and flushed. He loved this view more than anything else. The first time he ever saw it—her head tipped back, mouth slightly agape, a strand of damp hair caught on the edge of her lips—he knew just how lucky he was. He needed to hold onto her as long as he could.

Ten years on, she was only more spectacular. She was more womanly in some places, more toned and tight in others. She was so familiar, and yet as he saw her through the Castaway lens —the way audiences would see her, the way the other male contestants would see her—he finally couldn't hold back. It was with that forbidden thought that he finally came.

***

"YOU CAN WIN THIS," Andy said. They were standing on the front porch, waiting for the studio car to come and pick her up.

"I don't know." Back then, she was still filled with self-doubt. She hadn't emerged from the show with her confidence honed like hardened steel. "I'll try."

Andy knew that she would. She'd been training for this for months, and dreaming about it for so much longer. But there was one last piece of advice that he wanted to grant her, and he'd been rehearsing it for the last week. Rubbing his palms on his pants, he took a deep breath and launched into it. "Chels, listen. Don't talk about me on the show. Don't mention that you're married or seeing anyone."

Chelsea looked confused. She squirted up at him and said, "What?" like a jab.

"You've got everything it takes to win," he rambled. All the practice, all the time standing before a mirror, and this was still so hard to get out. "You're smart, strategic, and athletic. You can read people. You're gorgeous—"

She interrupted him. "Looking good isn't a requirement to win," she said, listing off in quick succession five past winners who weren't the prettiest or best looking.

"That's true, but listen," he said, persistent. "They're going to underestimate you, and... and guys will want to work with you." What he didn't tell her back then was that *he* wanted guys to work with her, too.

"You don't need to worry about me—"

"I'm not worried," he said, prepared for this retort, too. "It's just a month and change. You'll be back, and I don't want you to take anything off the table. If you need to pull a Felicity, go for it." Felicity, season 12's winner who used her beauty to get guys to do her bidding.

"I don't need to play that game to win," she said stubbornly.

"I know. You'll play your game, and it'll be amazing. You'll inspire a new generation of contestants."

Chelsea laughed at that.

Andy pressed on. He could be stubborn, too. "I'm just saying... don't take anything off the table, okay? I'll be here when you're back, no matter what. When you're out there, play to win. I... I want you to think of yourself as single, okay?"

She didn't say no, and when he slipped her rings free, she

didn't stop him, either. Chelsea didn't judge him. She didn't get angry. She'd just nodded, gave him one last kiss, and said, "I love you, Andy. I love you *so* much."

The network car pulled up. "I love you, too. Now go out there and live your dream."

She hugged him hard, one last time, turned, and slipped into the car. Holding her rings, he felt so alone and like such an idiot. Why was he playing with fire like this? He couldn't live without her. He squeezed them, feeling the diamond setting dig into his palm.

CHELSEA WAS GONE for just over six weeks. It was the longest that they'd been apart since they'd started dating ten years ago. Only absences were when one of them was traveling—for work or with friends—and for one of those trips to last longer than a week was unusual.

Those 46 days of separation were agonizing for Andy. At first, he treated it like she was just attending a conference. They were young, still in their mid-thirties, and had no kids and no pets. There was no one to come home to, so Andy just extended his work hours a little longer. He'd joined the gym with Chelsea as part of her training, and worked in visits with more frequency.

Otherwise, he picked something up on the way home and ate it in front of the TV, binging on Netflix and Amazon shows that he knew Chelsea had no interest in watching.

The routine worked for about a week. He remembered waking up one Saturday morning in an empty bed with an open and unplanned weekend before him. His social life was Chelsea. He didn't have any other close friends. He didn't have many activities outside of doing things with her, and now he had almost seven long weeks to fill without her.

The Castaways weren't allowed to communicate with the outside world other than during emergencies. Even if they were eliminated on the first day, they weren't allowed to come home because it would spoil the show.

The group was sequestered at a resort named Rescue for about a week where they underwent tests and training, met the Castaway film and production crew, and got acclimated to the Caribbean.

After that, they were brought by boat to the island, where the show was filmed for the next month. Everyone who was voted off went back to the resort, where they were again sequestered until all shooting was done and there were just three finalists. Votes were cast, but the winner was kept a secret until the live show, filmed months later. Finally, the Castaways were allowed to go home.

It was probably all a crazy whirlwind for Chelsea. For Andy, time crawled. He didn't experience any of the excitement of exotic locales and intense gamesmanship. He was alone, trying to pretend that everything was normal when nothing was.

So rather than pretend, he embraced the absence and dove deep in the world of Castaway. That early in filming and production, there was no web content for season 25. There weren't any contestant bios or clips. There wasn't even a teaser. So he watched older seasons, revisiting some of his favorite moments. Funny how much perceptions changed. As he watched the drama unfold and put his wife in all of those situations, it didn't feel like popcorn entertainment anymore.

Andy watched more than a few on-screen relationships blossom. Famously, in season 3, the winner and the runner-up ended up getting married. Other times, the attraction was a ruse, and the contestants talked about it in their private confessionals.

"I mean, James is cute and all," said Felicity from season 12, *"but*

this is a game. If he thinks I'm here for love, then..." Her grin was evil. *"...he'll never see me coming."*

At night, with the older episodes running through his head as he tossed and turned, he thought about Chelsea in those situations. He replayed their last moments together before the network car picked her up to take her to the airport.

Think of yourself as single.

Don't take anything off the table.

Pull a Felicity.

Every night, before falling asleep, he'd stare at her rings, which he kept in a dish beside the bed, just to remind himself that she would be home.

46 days. Just over six weeks. Andy could do it. He had the day of her return marked on the calendar: Saturday, March 2. He crossed out each day with a big, black Sharpie, and each day it got easier. He'd be fine. She'd be fine. Six weeks became five, which became four. The days moved more quickly. He stopped staring at those rings and worrying.

He'd keep his promise to her. He'd be there for her, no matter what.

3

CHELSEA'S RETURN

It was raining the day that Chelsea came home. Andy had been pacing the front hall of their modest home, unable to sit still, like he'd consumed a pot of coffee on a near empty stomach—which he'd also done.

He tried to focus on the rain outside, on what he'd say to her once he saw her again. He felt like he was meeting her for the first time, like this was a blind date. Like he had something to prove all over again.

When he heard the car door shut outside, his nerves spiked. A wave of heat and vertigo rushed up through him as he went to the door. Just over six weeks. 46 days. It had somehow felt like an eternity and the blink of an eye all at once.

Andy flung open the door to the rain, just in time to see her step out of the network car. A man was holding an umbrella for her like she was a movie star. In Andy's eyes, for one moment, she might as well have been.

Chelsea wore a belted raincoat that came to mid-thigh that he didn't recognize, and her gray, wool Allbirds that he did. Her caramel-brown hair was pulled back in a ponytail, but he could see the golden highlights she had from all her time in the sun.

It was her face that he couldn't get past, though. She'd lost weight in the last month, sharpening her cheekbones and chin. Coupled with the rich tan she wore, he barely recognized her, and he felt shy when he met her eyes.

A second man trailed the one with the umbrella, carrying her bags to the front door.

"Where would you like them, miss?" he asked. Chelsea didn't seem to hear him. She was just as dumb-struck as Andy, staring at him, the air between them charged.

"Andy," she mouthed, although no sound came out.

The porter cleared his throat. Andy stepped aside, gesturing vaguely to the left. "Right there is fine."

"Thanks," Chelsea said. Her voice sounded huskier, like a cold was coming on.

The man left her bags where Andy had instructed, nodded at the two of them, and left, pulling the door shut.

"You... have a good flight?" Andy asked.

Chelsea was having none of that. She stepped up to him, cupped his head in her hands, and pulled him in for a searing kiss. Absence makes the heart grow fonder, and desire grow even hotter. With that kiss, the plug was pulled and all the pent up desires and emotions came rushing in.

They made out on their way to the bedroom, something that they'd literally never done. Like a movie, they left a trail of clothing up the stairs—Chelsea's new raincoat and old shoes, Andy's hoodie, his socks, his jeans left limp on the top step.

Beneath the coat, Chelsea wore an oversized sweatshirt that reminded him of her younger years, and skintight leggings that were nothing like those years.

When Chelsea pulled his shirt off and her eyes roamed his bare chest, he felt self-conscious. She'd spent the last month with young, fit men who walked around shirtless most of the time. How could he hold up next to all that brawn?

She traced his pecs with her fingers before looking up at him. "You look *good*, Andy. Have you been working out?"

"One of the few things I filled my time with."

She sank her teeth into her bottom lip and nodded in approval. "Definitely keep it up. I love it."

When she pulled her sweatshirt off, she didn't have any such bashfulness or insecurity. Beneath, she wore a familiar green bra that lifted her tits into a nice valley of tanned cleavage. She'd definitely lost weight while on the island. He could see her ribs now, and she was more lean muscle than soft curves. This felt surreal, like some kind of dream, and at any moment he'd wake up and he'd be alone again.

But like his whole life with Chelsea, he'd savor every moment until that waking. They came back together, kissing hard, hands refamiliarizing each other. She wasn't wearing anything beneath her leggings, he realized as he cupped her ass, and he confirmed it a moment later when she was on the bed and he started to pull them off.

She had tan lines now, pale triangles over her breasts and down around her waist. He'd forgotten about the laser hair removal, and gasped at the sight of her smooth mound.

She stopped him before he dove down between her thighs, though. "No," she said, her hand on his chin. "I don't need that right now. I *need* to get fucked."

It wasn't a thing that Chelsea usually said—not unless she was really horny. Judging from her hard nipples, her ragged breathing, her slippery pussy, she was really horny. Andy obliged, even harder now, even more turned on. Climbing up her body, he felt her fingers curl around his dick and guide him to her sex.

"Uhnn!" she cried out, pulling him down to her, his body against hers. She dug her nails into his back as he sank his dick in. It was exquisite. After a month and a half of nothing but his hand, feeling her warm snatch nearly set him off.

Chelsea got there first. "Yes, this!" she cried. "Give it to me, Andy. Fuck me. FUCK ME!"

She lifted her knees to either side of him, spreading her legs open as Andy rammed his dick deep. Despite all the trips to the gym, his buttocks ached and his abs screamed as he fucked her.

"Andy... oh, Andy! Oh! Oh!"

Chelsea mauled his back, raking her nails along his shoulder blades. They'd *never* had sex like this. She'd never needed it so hard, even in their newlywed days. Now—

"Are you close, baby? I need your come. Give me your come!"

"Chels... oh..." He wanted to cling to the moment, to the reunion, to the confidence in knowing that right now, he was all that she wanted. But nothing lasts forever, and he couldn't hold out. "Uhhh!"

He was there with her, going dizzy as he drove into her one final time, sinking to the hilt. After weeks without sex, this orgasm came on like a tsunami, relentlessly battering him with waves of ecstasy.

Chelsea wasn't done. She needed more, and before Andy was fully recovered, she was pushing him onto his back and diving down between his legs. Her mouth on his wilting cock tore a groan from him.

"That's... ha..." It was too much, but who was he to turn down a spontaneous blowjob?

Chelsea remained focused on getting him hard again, pumping him with her hand and mouth at once. Despite that, she could only get him up about halfway.

That was until he thought about her time on the island. He thought about the older seasons that he'd watched, about the flirtations caught on film, the alliances between men and women that were only sort of platonic. It sometimes got cold at night on the island. Did Chelsea snuggle up to some other guy when it did? Just for warmth at first, maybe, but later, for more?

And just like that, he was hard again, filling Chelsea's mouth until she was satisfied. She crawled up beside him, kissing him as she jerked his dick, but didn't straddle him as usual. "Round two?" she asked, positioning herself on her hands and knees.

Doggystyle? It wasn't a position they did much but for no real reason other than that it was out of their routine. It got Andy wondering why she was breaking their routine.

"Round two, yes," he said, moving into place behind her. "And round three and four if we can get there. We've got a lot of time to make up for."

Chelsea's giggle turned into a gasp as he fed his dick back into her from behind. He was harder than ever, fueled by the troubling thought that maybe he wasn't the first guy to fuck her like this since she'd left.

"Yes, Andy! You feel so... hard!"

He ran his eyes over her undulating body. Despite four weeks of being malnourished, she still had her curves—the way her heart-shaped ass narrowed at her waist before flaring back with her ribs and now sinewy shoulders. He ran his hand up her spine, tracing the channel from tailbone to shoulder blades. She groaned, wiggling her hips and pushing back into him.

The angle felt so good, different than normal. From behind, he could fuck her deeper, reach places he normally couldn't. She felt tighter this way, too, her pussy squeezing his cock at the base, squeezing as he withdrew, trying to forbid him from leaving her.

He'd already come once. It gave him the ability to fuck longer, although his muscles screamed. This was harder than any time on the elliptical or the stationary bike. But he wasn't going to relent. Not with Chelsea moaning like a fucking pornstar.

"Fuck me! Fuck me, Andy! Yes!"

It was so hot. So ripe. He held her hips and fucked her as she got wetter and wetter, the sounds of sex sloshing through a bedroom that had long been quiet—even before she went away.

Before he came again, he swore that Chelsea had orgasmed at least twice. He felt great. He felt like a sex god in a way that he never had before. And why not? This woman was a goddess—and he got her all to himself.

That was right, right?

In the doubt, he popped, emptying what remained into her juicy sex. She groaned, too, throaty and raw. They collapsed into a spoon, his dick still buried in her as they both fought to catch their breath.

"Wow," Andy said. Her hair smelled clean. After spending so much time on the beach without amenities, being clean must have been a novel thing for her. Or maybe not. Maybe she'd been the first to get eliminated. Maybe she'd spent the last six weeks in a resort, joined every few days by a new—and inevitably attractive—contestant who'd just been cast off.

With that running through his head, he asked, "So are we millionaires now?"

Chelsea laughed. She shifted, and his dick finally slipped free. They found themselves on their backs, fingers touching, staring at the ceiling, just like old times. "First of all, no one knows the winner. We don't find out until the live show, which is three months away. And secondly, I couldn't tell you even if I was one of the finalists. I'm not supposed to tell you anything."

Andy turned onto his side, propping his head on his arm. Chelsea seemed to purposely not look at him. He wondered about how much she'd tell him about the experience. "Not even a hint?"

"Nope," she said, shaking her head. "Only thing I'm allowed to say is that I did participate on the show."

"You were gone long enough, I sure hope you did!" He kissed her. "So nothing else?'

She glanced at him out of the corner of her eyes. "You'll have to watch, like the rest of the world."

"That's no fun."

She turned to face him, propping her head up on her elbow. It felt like a sleepover. "Well, if the editors are any good, it should be a lot of fun. It was a good group we had out there." He heard the wistfulness in her voice, like the way some people got talking about college. When she saw him watching her, the wistfulness was gone. In the background, they could hear the rain on their roof. "You know what's amazing?"

"Hmm?"

"Being able to lie here with it raining and not have to worry about our makeshift shelter leaking." She flopped onto her back, stretching her arms above her head. "I could do this all day long."

Andy ran his hand up the side of her body, cupping her breast. "Sounds fun. Want to try?"

Chelsea laughed. She spotted her rings on the bedside table, scooped them up, and slipped them back onto her fingers. They fit perfectly. Splaying her hand above her, she said, "It's so good to be home. I missed you so much, Andy."

"Welcome home, Chels." He kissed her, but they were back to the familiar, married kiss. "I'm *so* glad you're home."

4

THE BUILDUP

The show didn't start airing until a month after Chelsea's return, which, given the polished production, was pretty good. In the run-up, the website published short video bios on each of the sixteen contestants. Andy watched them all, although at the time, they really were strangers.

He watched Chelsea's first, of course, and even that one almost felt like watching a stranger who looked like his wife. They had her sitting on a beach with the ocean stretched out behind her. Her hair was loose, catching in the breeze. She wore a pair of metal-framed librarian glasses that Andy had never seen her wear before—doubly odd since she'd had laser eye surgery.

These videos were always shot before the game began, when everyone was clean and bright and unprepared for what came next.

"Hi, I'm Chelsea from Philadelphia," she introduced herself. Chelsea herself refused to watch any of this. Back then, she was too embarrassed to see herself on camera, and even as they watched the first episode together, she'd spent most of the time

hiding beneath a blanket. *"I'm 33. I'm a librarian at the National Constitution Center. I guess one of the things I love about my job is sorting and organizing everything that comes in. That's going to be my approach with this game. If I understand where everyone else fits into the game, hopefully that'll give me an edge."*

This was Chelsea, her greatest strength, and potentially her greatest weakness. People weren't books to be categorized to be understood, especially when they were all coming with agendas. Andy had tried to coach her to think that way.

"I'm definitely an introvert, preferring to be around my books." Her laugh was so cute, and like old times, she adjusted her glasses on the bridge of her nose. *"I'm hoping that Castaway will help me get out of my shell some. I've been training hard for the physical challenges, but it's the social element that... I just don't know."*

She hid her face in her hands as she laughed nervously. The video cut to her in a more composed state as it wrapped up. *"I've been a fan since the first season. I can't wait to play, and I'm bringing it all. Hopefully they'll see this shy librarian and not see the real threat before it's too late."*

Interspersed through the interview were scenes from the show, snippets of B-roll to give the viewers a sense of what was to come. Andy studied those more closely than he did her words. Of course, he didn't know anyone at the time, but he saw her laughing with her ally, Kim. There was footage of her leaping into the water wearing her pale pink bikini. Any time there was another guy in the B-roll, though, Andy felt a jolt of nervous excitement.

Watching the rest of the videos, it was clear that almost everyone there was chosen not just for their diverse stories and backgrounds, but also how well they'd present on television.

Andy was biased, but he thought Chelsea was the most beautiful contestant this season. Being forced to see her the way the network presented her to the world, he really realized how lucky he was.

Others gave her a run for her money, though. Brooklyn, a blonde from Texas who was identified as a former cheerleader, was hot in a more generic way. Kim, the petite redhead and later Chelsea's friend, was cute and spunky. Janice was the oldest woman on the show at 44, and in the interview she worried that everyone would see her as the old and vulnerable member. It's funny how relative age was, and how cruel media could be, particularly to women. Her "profession" was "Divorcee," which just felt inherently wrong to Andy. Like all the rest, though, she was hot with her bob of short brown hair, her lithe body, her (probably) enhanced tits.

The guys were equally fun eye candy for those looking, covering the gamut of romance novel stereotypes. There was Todd, the Fireman, Kyle, the gym-going investment banker, Isaiah the young personal trainer. Andy glossed past most, other than thinking about all those buff dudes spending an extended time with Chelsea in a tropical paradise.

5

EPISODE 1

The first episode aired about a month after Chelsea returned from location. They watched it together, cuddled on the sofa in the dark, snuggling beneath a blanket. It was almost like it was before she'd left, although Andy could feel the change. He wondered if things would ever be the same.

"Wait, why are you wearing glasses?" he asked as "Chelsea, The Librarian" was introduced on the customary ship as it headed for the "deserted" island, along with the other 16 contestants. Molly Reynolds was there, getting to know the large cast by firing off questions.

Chelsea wore a pale pink blouse and a cardigan, an absurd outfit for a deserted beach, along with a pair of roundish, metal-framed, granny glasses.

She said, "They told me it fit the librarian persona for me."

"But... you got LASIK..." Andy didn't get it.

"The glasses were fake. Not corrective. They were just for effect. I also don't wear cardigans like that. And Melody on the end there doesn't really wear flowy dresses, but her persona was 'hippy chick.' Mine was 'nerd girl librarian.'" She shrugged. "It's part of the fiction."

"So, like, is any of this real?" Andy asked

"The show? The contest? Definitely. The competitions were real. Most stuff happened, just..." And here's the thing that stuck with Andy as he watched all twelve episodes of Castaway. "...don't believe all of the drama. A lot of that is creative editing."

On the show, Molly pointed at Chelsea. *"Tall woman with the glasses, how are you feeling right now?"*

Beside me, Chelsea laid it out. "See, that's how they boiled me down to at first." She giggled, good-natured about it all. "Tall Woman With The Glasses. At least it wasn't like my high school gym teacher—big girl with braces."

On screen, Tall Girl With The Glasses answered the question. *"Right now, honestly, I'm feeling overdressed."* The rest of the contestants laughed as she plucked at her cardigan.

"Go ahead and take it off," Molly said. *"Out here, on Castaway, it's time to leave your old life behind."*

Chelsea looked uncertain about what she was supposed to do as she unbuttoned the cardigan. The pale pink blouse beneath was sleeveless, baring her toned arms which were already starting to brown from the sun. Then, in an act of pure impulse, she threw the cardigan over the side of the ship, into the choppy waters below.

Even Molly Reynolds seemed surprised. *"Okay, yes! Shed it all, girl."* She pointed to a man who the screen introduced as Todd, The Fireman, but who Molly addressed as, *"Guy with the blue uniform, with the tattoos. What do you think about that?"*

Todd looked over at Chelsea and grinned. *"She can leave more of her past behind if she wants to."*

The contestants laughed. Molly rolled her eyes, but smiled. When the camera switched to Chelsea, she was blushing, but didn't curl up into a ball. *"And you?"* Molly probed. *"Are you ready to come out here and play for a million dollars?"*

Todd, The Fireman, answered confidently. *"Past, future, present. I'm always ready to play."*

6

EPISODE 5

The first time that Todd and Chelsea started working together, in secret, came in the fifth episode. Andy would rewatch it again, later, when its full significance became clear. Even in the moment, though, it was visceral.

Chelsea's closest ally at the beginning, Kim, had left the game the previous episode. What she didn't know at the time, but what the editing made clear, was that the others were scared of Chelsea. They saw the tall, quiet librarian as a threat and wanted to neutralize her early on.

Chelsea was sitting alone on the beach, staring out at the horizon, wearing nothing but her bra and boy-short panties. By episode 5, Andy was *almost* desensitized to this state of undress.

Todd came along and took a seat beside her. He was shirtless, too, although mercifully he wore his trousers, which were already frayed at the cuffs. *"Hey, you okay?"*

Chelsea took a deep breath and turned to him as if just noticing him for the first time. *"Honestly? No. This sucks."*

"It's hard when you don't see it coming," Todd agreed. *"For what it's worth, I didn't write Kim's name down."*

"And I'm supposed to believe that?" Chelsea was in a really bitter mood.

"No, but I hope that you do."

They sat there quietly. The show cut to a different camera, shot from out wide, showing the two of them alone on the wide swath of beautiful beach.

It was Todd who spoke at last. *"You looking for another partner?"*

"I don't know. I don't think I can do this much longer. These people... it's all so... <bleep> hard." Chelsea clapped her hand over her mouth and laughed. *"I'm sorry."*

Todd put an arm around her, and Chelsea turned into his embrace, letting herself be hugged—hugging him back.

For Andy, at home, that hug felt like the realization of his worst nightmares and most intense fantasies. They were friends, but also not. He'd not paid much attention to Todd until then. Now he did. The fireman was a handsome guy in a gritty, working class kind of way. He had tattoos up and down his arms and partially across his right shoulder. His muscle-hewn upper body was hairless other than a trail from his navel down into his pants. He had a square jaw, a nose that looked like it had been broken once or twice, and looked good with a week of growth on his face.

Worst of all, he looked good with Chelsea and her tall, dark beauty. Andy could imagine that hug turning into something more. Chelsea in her bra, her full tits compressing against that bare chest, only fueled the fantasy.

It didn't go there, of course. The hug ended without more affection. It was supportive, yet the editing work suggested that maybe it was more. It captured Chelsea's blush, and Todd's furtive look into her cleavage. It captured the awkward clearing of throats between the two of them.

Andy looked at Chelsea on the sofa beside him. Was she

flushed now? He couldn't quite tell in the dark, and when she felt his eyes on her, she shifted over to him. "The editing makes it look like more than it is," she said.

"It's okay." They were the right words for Andy to say at the time, but also a huge lie.

Back on screen...

"*Let's work together,*" Todd continued. "*But in secret. People see partnerships as threats, and here's the thing—no one'll see us coming. No one will suspect. The fireman and the librarian? It's perfect.*"

"*Okay, let's do it. What do I have to lose?*"

The show cut to an interview with her alone on a different stretch of beach. She looked more relaxed now, less forlorn. "*Do I trust Todd? No. I don't trust anyone. Trust needs to be earned, not freely given, and right now, all anyone's been able to do is lose it. But right now, I'm going to keep my options open, and see where this one goes.*"

After that episode, Andy dove into Todd's background. He went back and watched the intro video of him more carefully—fireman from LA, 35-years-old, single, used to be in the army, then joined CAL FIRE to battle in California before "settling down" with the Los Angeles Fire Department.

"*Everyone's going to see me as a physical threat, but I've got social game,*" he said, adding with a grin, "*Especially with the ladies.*" His followup laugh wasn't one of embarrassment.

7

———

ALLIANCES AND BETRAYALS

As the season progressed, Todd earned Chelsea's trust, alerting her to a possible vote against her that she was able to avert. Secretly, he armed her with information that she could use to manipulate to their advantage. It helped that Brooklyn and Kyle's very open relationship—and to a lesser extent, the two gay guys David and Harry's—were focusing most of the attention on them.

The internet didn't miss Chelsea and Todd's secret alliance, though. Andy spent a lot of time on the Castaway subreddit, where there were whole threads each week dedicated to them. Andy would obsess over those posts, torturing himself as he pored over them, jerking off over them when he was alone.

"Chelsea and Todd should just get it on already. They clearly both want it!"

"I know this sub loves BrooKyle, but I'm all in on whatever the fuck's going on with Todd and Chelsea. Love all the tension."

"It's like one of the best RomComs—opposites attracting, everyone knows that they should get together except for them until the very end. It's delicious!"

Reading that stuff, the virtual cuckold shame was real, and yet he couldn't stop reading it, again and again, week after week. He was saved from having to deal with it in real life, though, for the most part. The people that he worked with didn't care about the reality TV game show, he wasn't close with his family, and didn't have any close friends.

He did wonder about Chelsea's work, though. They almost certainly watched it, if only out of curiosity about where she'd been for six weeks. Did they tease her, too? Did they have the guts that Andy lacked, asking her what was up with her and Todd?

But he didn't have the guts, and Chelsea wasn't volunteering any insight beyond what was aired. She leaned heavily on the NDA that she'd signed, and how she wasn't allowed to share anything.

Still, he couldn't help but notice that she was always down for sex after watching an episode. He wondered what she was thinking about behind her closed eyes, and secretly hoped that she was thinking about Todd.

AND THEN, episode 11 arrived, one of the most consequential and talked about episodes in Castaway history. Only five remained. Chelsea and Todd were now openly working with one another, and were in a strong position to make it into the final three. Just one last hurdle. But this was when paranoia set in. It's what made Castaway such a success despite being on for so many years. There was only one winner. Even the strongest alliance could crumble in the end.

"I will never vote to cast you away," Chelsea told Todd.

The cinematography couldn't have been better. Up there on

Andy and Chelsea's large television, the cameraman had the scene framed perfectly—the two sitting on the beach as the sun set, alone and bathed in orange light and shadow.

Andy watched, enraptured, along with the rest of the viewing nation. Only he had Chelsea at his side—the real Chelsea, back from the game, shifting beside him and refusing to look his way.

On screen, Todd answered Chelsea's commitment with his own. *"And you know I won't write yours down, Chels."*

Andy squeezed the real Chelsea's hand. "It's okay," Andy told her. "I'm okay."

"Andy, I..." He hated how guilty this made her, especially as he sat there with his own confused excitement.

"Seriously, Chelsea, I get it. You like him."

"I liked playing the game with him." It was a knee jerk clarification. Andy knew it, but left it alone, turning back to the television.

They both knew that there was more to it than that, but both left it alone, turning back to the television.

"We can do this," Todd said. On screen, Chelsea looked at Todd as he looked off at the setting sun. It wasn't gamesmanship in her eyes, but genuine affection. When he turned to her, she averted her gaze down into her hands. *"We make it through this next vote and we should be able to walk into the final."*

The show cut to a confessional—Chelsea sitting on a log with a stretch of white sand behind her. *"I don't know what to do."* There was emotion in her face. *"They are coming for us. If I stick with this alliance, it could be me going home. But if I vote for him, I lose my closest ally and... "*

She didn't finish the sentence, instead looking away from the camera and shaking her head.

"I don't know what to do," she repeated before the scene cut to Todd's much more optimistic beach confessional.

"We've got this. Chelsea and I are going to go down as the greatest couple on Castaway." He grinned. *"Not that we're actually a couple, but hey, a guy can dream, right?"*

As Andy watched the series of scenes play out, it felt like someone had fastened a belt around his chest and was slowly tightening it. It became hard to breathe. He started to feel dizzy. It wasn't entirely unwelcome.

"He likes you," Andy said. When he looked over at Chelsea, she was flushed. Before she could deny it, he moved on. "You know, that's pretty... cool." He was going to say 'hot' or 'exciting' but chickened out. "It's got to feel good knowing a guy like that's got the hots for you."

"And you know what?" she asked, crawling into Andy's lap. "He doesn't get me." She wrapped her arms around him. "You do."

They started making out as the show rolled on in the background. Both of them forgot all about it, the inevitable outcome. Chelsea wore a gray, ribbed top that was not only tight over her full chest, but scooped low enough in the front to display more cleavage than she'd ever shown before the show.

Beneath that, she wore a new bra that she'd purchased since coming back. She'd replaced most of her lingerie since then, and Andy was loving it. This one was lacy white with pink and yellow flowers at the fringes, and did an excellent job pushing her tits together.

"How are you still so tanned?" Andy asked, admiring the contrast of white against her bronzed skin.

Sheepishly, she admitted, "I've been going to a tanning bed. I know, I know, it's terrible, but the live show finale is in two weeks."

"Is it bad to say that I love it?"

She ran her hands over his shoulders, caressing his neck. It wasn't hard to wonder if she was doing this to compare him with

Todd, and it was even easier for Andy to conclude that he'd come up short in that comparison. That feeling of inadequacy fueled his lust for her even more.

He kissed her, running his fingers down her smooth body. His cock thickened, and she had to have felt it there against her knee.

Tanning wasn't the only change that he'd noticed in the last three months. Since the show, she'd gotten herself back up to a healthier weight, although she now jogged every morning and was more regimented at the gym and in her diet. The results were undeniable. She was in the best shape of her life.

The question that wormed its way into Andy again and again was: who was she looking good for? Herself, most likely, and also for him, for an audience eager to see her again on the live show... but also, for Todd?

He kissed her harder. He grabbed her ass, tugging at the waistband of her tight leggings. She wore a matching thong beneath, cleaving her ass and highlighting just how good her round butt was. He filled his hands with those cheeks, squeezing her, drawing her closer to him as their kiss deepened even more.

She grabbed his shirt, clawing to get it off, to feel his skin against her own. Efficiently, she reached behind her back and twisted open her bra, shrugging it open Andy kicked off his pants and boxers.

She didn't take her thong off. She couldn't wait any longer. She just pushed it to the side, grabbed his cock, and sank down on it. Andy held her closer, her pillowy tits against his chest as she rode him.

Behind her, the final discussion before voting was happening. Molly Reynolds was asking probing questions, getting the five remaining contestants to reveal how they were feeling and who would be going out. Andy was only vaguely listening until he heard something Chelsea said on screen.

"...what you don't realize watching this on TV is how real these emotions are."

"Tell me more about that," Molly probed.

On-screen Chelsea answered. *"Like, when you're not part of all this, it seems so easy to know the right way to play, or the right strategies at the moment. But at home, you're only seeing one limited angle, and you're not feeling what we all feel. The five of us... we're all close. They're like family."*

Andy looked past Chelsea, towards the TV just as it cut over to Todd, who was watching her and nodding. The camera cut back to a grimier version of Chelsea. She was wearing the pale, pink blouse that she wore from the beginning, now tied beneath her breasts, leaving her stomach bare.

"How do you decide to cast away your family?" she asked. Whether it was editing and splicing footage together smartly, when the camera cut to a closer shot of her face, weary from spending weeks on the beach, she seemed to be looking at Todd. And her eyes were full of sadness as she did so.

Andy tightened his hands on Chelsea's ass. His cuck angst grew, and his dick swelled with it. "Ah, Andy!" Chelsea cried, tossing her head back. She bounced on him faster, oblivious to the show now. Oblivious to the emotions that she'd once had, or the ones roiling Andy now.

On screen, each player got up to write down a name. They *had* to write a name. That was the rub. They were family, but in the end, one of the family needed to go. On-screen Chelsea looked so forlorn as she scribbled down a name that the camera wouldn't show, frowning. When she returned to her seat, she wouldn't meet Todd's eyes.

"Uh!" Andy's balls seized. He tried to hold back. He tried to last just a little longer. "Oh, Chels..."

"Andy!"

Beyond her, Molly Reynolds reviewed the votes. *"It's always tough when we get to this part of the game. You've had a good run, but you've been cast away..."* She paused for dramatic effect. Chelsea was bouncing hard in his lap, and Andy was only half able to focus. *"...Todd."*

Everyone gasped, on the show and in living rooms across America. On screen, those who were cast away previously, and who'd ultimately decide the winner, were also shocked. Chelsea had turned on her closest ally.

"Andy!" she gasped, back in the present. "Andy, come. Come!"

She ground her hips into his lap, taking all of him into her as she squeezed her head and drew him against her chest. Tossing her head, she came hard.

Behind her, Andy saw another version of his wife stand in her seat as Todd gathered his things. She was hurt. She was in pain. She took him into her arms as the camera panned in. *"I'm so sorry,"* she said to him, so quietly that the show displayed the subtitles at the bottom of the screen. *"So, so sorry..."*

At first, it didn't look like Todd would return the hug. He looked just as stunned as everyone else. But that hesitation only lasted a moment. He grinned, folding his tattoo-sleeved arms around her.

"We could have gone all the way, Chels," he said. Again, the subtitles were there. *"Good luck."*

Andy came before the on-screen hug ended. It felt like being struck by lightning. It was like every jolt he'd felt as he watched the show, every spark and sizzle that traveled along his spine, had been balled up into one bright-white bolt of energy. His whole body seized. He rocked backwards on the sofa, thrusting his hips up into Chelsea. He held her hips as the world went woozy. He came and came, emptying all that stored up angst into his wife.

The show was in a commercial by the time he crawled back

to some form of sanity. Chelsea was still there, huffing and gasping over him, her body draped over his. He held her close. She was real. She was solid. And she was with him still.

Chelsea was right. In the end, Todd didn't get her. Andy did. But that didn't stop Andy from wondering, as always, what if...

8

———

EPISODE 12

The penultimate episode aired a week before they were to travel to LA for the finale—the episode in which Chelsea was finally cast away, the fourth and final member of the voting crew.

Andy didn't know that, of course. He watched from the edge of his seat as the final four played a game of paranoia and deception. As an outside observer, it was obvious that the only two real players left who could win the votes of the castaways was Jason or Chelsea.

He asked her about that as they watched episode 12. "Did those other two know that they were just being taken along because they couldn't win?"

Chelsea didn't answer. She didn't even acknowledge the question. She looked white as a sheet, eyes wide, staring at the television while somehow not seeing it.

"You okay?" he asked.

She realized that he was talking to her, and snapped out of her daze. "Yeah, I'm... what did you ask?"

"Just that it's you or Jason here."

"Oh, yeah. I think we knew it, but you never want to tell

someone else that they can't win. You need to pump up their egos and downplay your own." She said it so matter-of-factly, like she'd been manipulating people her whole life.

They watched the final physical challenge, a long obstacle course that ended in a life size slide puzzle. Whoever won this would be guaranteed a spot in the finale, and as things seemed to be going, Morgan needed to win. Jason had already convinced the other two that she was the biggest threat.

Andy held Chelsea's hand as she raced through the course. Her hand was just as clammy as his, her body just as tense, even knowing the outcome.

Chelsea had the edge over Jason. She'd won three other immunities before this moment. She was good at puzzles. She flew through the course, arriving at the puzzle first. But one of the others was right on her heels, and in a critical misstep, Chelsea fell behind.

"You've got this," Andy whispered from the couch. "You've—"

But she didn't. She was a step too slow. Molly Reynolds declared the other contestant the winner, Chelsea slammed her hands on the puzzle in frustration.

"Damn," Andy swore. "I thought you had that!"

He had started to believe that she actually was one of the finalists, and that when they took the trip out to LA next week, it was to see if they were newly millionaires. He figured that was why she was being so cagey. Without the safety of immunity, Chelsea's time was over.

Even still, the show did a masterful job keeping him on edge, right through the votes. Despite it seeming like Jason had everyone in his pocket, Andy stayed on edge, right up until Molly announced that she'd been cast away.

"I'm sorry, Chels. I thought you had that."

When he finally looked away from the television, he found

Chelsea sitting quietly beside him, wringing her hands, her face pale despite all the trips to the tanning bed.

A pit formed in Andy's gut. Something bad was brewing.

"What is it, honey? Everything okay?"

When she didn't immediately smile and dismiss it with the wave of her hand, his blood pressure rose and his chest tightened. This wasn't just about her getting voted off. For Chelsea, that moment happened months ago. This was something else.

Chelsea couldn't even meet his eyes at first. She took a shallow breath, squeezed her fingers together, and said, "I need to tell you something."

At last, her eyes met his, and it was like he'd been rocketed into the stratosphere, where the air was thin, where he couldn't breathe fast enough. Giddy and defensive, he made a dumb joke. He leaned in and said, "You fucked Todd."

Just uttering those words felt like a rush, his stomach rising into his throat, the thin air of his imagined stratosphere dropping away as he plummeted. Even though he knew that wasn't it —that it *couldn't* be it—stating his greatest fear and fantasy aloud felt so dangerous.

Then he saw her face, the look of surprise, the way her mouth parted and her eyes went wide with fear. She said, "How...?"

"Wait." No. No, no. He pinched the bridge of his nose. "You really did?"

"Not....exactly. But something did happen..."

Oh, God, oh God!

"...on the last night at Rescue." A tear rolled down her cheek. "I'm... I'm so sorry."

9

LAST DAY AT RESCUE

"It felt like the final day of college, you know?" Chelsea began. They'd shut the TV off, and Andy had refilled their glasses of wine. Chelsea sat stiffly on the edge of the sofa, staring into her glass as she gave what felt like a final confession. "We were saying goodbye to our friends and acquaintances, knowing that we may never see some of them again. I know it sounds weird, since we weren't together for that long, but it was still…"

"I get it, Chels. You all had an intense experience together. Makes sense to me."

"It wasn't just the other contestants, but the crew as well. There was this one producer, Camila, who I basically talked to every day that I was there. She was the only one I told about you, but I needed that release valve, and… and it was sad to say goodbye to her." She shook her head. "But it was more than that. It was saying goodbye to the whole production, the whole experience. There were definitely things I was happy to leave behind, like feeling dirty and hungry and paranoid every waking moment, but you know what? That was part of it, too."

"It was the experience, all of it," Andy said.

"Yes." Chelsea took a deep breath. "Okay, so that last night…"

THAT LAST NIGHT, they'd gotten together as a group and had one large, final meal. Drinks flowed. Food was consumed. Everyone congratulated the finalists. Some attempted to bury bad blood, anticipating some of what would be aired when the show went live. Tensions that existed from the beginning were put on hold for one night as everyone let their hair down.

Chelsea was feeling good as she floated away from the main group. She'd been forced to live with all these people for the last month, and for an introvert, that was exhausting. As much as she didn't want this to end, she was looking forward to getting home and seeing Andy.

Rescue was a nice resort villa. Located on a more populated island, the Castaway headquarters was closer to the tropical paradise that Chelsea expected when she thought about the Caribbean. The three story villa had a beautiful pool in the courtyard, balconies all over the place, a well-kept lawn that tapered out to a long, white sandy beach.

Chelsea had explored the space in the last few days since she'd been cast off. It gave her space to be by herself and be alone. She sought that now, although she was torn. This was a time to be with people. To enjoy these last moments.

Deciding to grab something from her room, she turned away from the view of the evening grounds and the solace that it offered and headed back inside, winding her way through the grounds to her wing of the villa. Unfamiliar with the space, she got turned around and lost. Just as she realized that she was in the wrong part of the resort, she heard it.

A woman's unmistakable cry of pleasure. Chelsea's body reacted like a starving woman seeing a plate of food for the first time in weeks. She hadn't had sex since Andy, and hadn't dared even touch herself while she was still on the show. Now, she was drawn to this sound, which took her right to an open door on the top floor of this very building.

"Uh! Uh! Uh!" Definitely a woman, definitely having sex. She could hear the wet slapping of skin on skin.

Chelsea knew this went on at the resort. There were readily available condoms in all of the bedrooms, and she'd heard whispered rumors of cast and crew hooking up. She hadn't asked anyone about it, being a private person herself, but she *was* curious. So curious. Curious enough that she tip-toed right up to the edge of the doorway and looked in.

She recognized Kyle immediately. Like most of the guys on the show, Kyle had tattoos. His were understated, but she'd come to see the yin-yang tattoo on his right shoulder as part of his surfer-guy persona. That and the shaggy locks of golden hair that fell around his chin. He was hot, and she'd looked at his chiseled upper body with hungry curiosity more than once.

Seeing him, she expected to see his showmance girlfriend, Brooklyn, in bed with him. And she was, she just wasn't being fucked by Kyle. No, she was beside him, on her hands and knees, as one of the *other* contestants, Isaiah, a 22-year-old black personal trainer from Chicago, fucked her from behind.

But that wasn't the most shocking thing that Chelsea saw as she looked into the room. No, that came when Brooklyn shifted slightly, giving Chelsea a glimpse of the woman Kyle was fucking. There, on her back with her dark hair damp with perspiration, was the host and showrunner, Molly Reynolds.

"Fuck her, Kyle," Brooklyn encouraged. Her own blond tresses were still back in a ponytail and her forehead was dappled with sweat. "I know how much you've wanted it."

Brooklyn was playing with Molly's tits, tweaking the other woman's dark nipples as she came loudly.

"That's it, baby. Fuck her. She's so hot when she comes." With that statement, Brooklyn leaned over and kissed Molly on the lips. It was neither unwelcome nor unexpected, as Molly quickly returned the kiss, her hand curling behind the blond's neck to pull her even closer.

"Aw, hell yeah!" Isaiah moaned. He brushed his hand along Brooklyn's ass as he buried his dick to his balls and came.

Chelsea couldn't believe what she was seeing. She'd only watched a few pornos and had never seen other people having sex before, let alone a foursome. Abstractly, she knew that these sorts of things happened, but until she saw it with her own eyes, she never really believed it.

It was one of the hottest things she'd ever seen. She practically shook with lust as she listened to their moans of release. She wondered what that must feel like and instantly craved that feeling. She watched Brooklyn and Molly come and wanted more than anything to feel that.

When Isaiah pulled his cock free, Chelsea's mouth fell open. That black dick was huge, even limp, burdened by his used condom. At the same time, Kyle pulled his own dick free of the Castaway host, and while his dick wasn't quite as large, it was big enough to make Chelsea gasp. She clapped her hand over her mouth, her face burning with the fear of discovery. The foursome didn't see her. They were so focused on Kyle as he tore the condom off and came all over Molly's washboard stomach and smooth, hair-free mound.

Brooklyn crawled down between Molly's legs, their eyes meeting before she started to lick her boyfriend's come off of the older woman. Isaiah grinned, stretching his arms over his head. He started to turn towards the door.

Chelsea ducked back just in time, her nerves jolting, every pore in her body crackling with electricity. Shit. Shit, shit. That was too close.

"Get that dick up here, Isaiah," she heard Molly say. "Fuck my face while this slut eats me out."

Was this really the host she'd admired for so many years? She didn't hate the discovery, no matter how shocking.

"Mmm, yes," Molly slurped. "This may be the best... season... yet..."

Chelsea was away before she was tempted back in. Her nerves couldn't settle. Breathing became difficult. Even walking felt erratic. She was so horny. So fucking horny. Before she knew it, she was back to the hall where she was staying, where she'd meant to go in the first place.

All she could think about was getting inside and burying her fingers in her pussy. She was so singularly focused on it that she literally ran into Todd.

"Chels!" he said, catching her. She was vaguely aware that his hair was wet and he wasn't wearing a shirt. Over the last month, on the show, this seemed so normal. Here, in the resort, societal norms were slowly returning, but she wasn't there yet. "You look like you saw a ghost. Everything okay?"

"Yeah, I..." The scene was still so raw, burned into her brain. She couldn't speak. She could still see their naked bodies, see the muscles, the men, the cocks.

Todd mistook her shock as some kind of trauma. He gathered her in his arms, saying, "Hey, hey..."

His arms were strong, his body as solid as the side of a mountain. This man was a fireman, and embodied that stereotype in all the sexiest of ways. Chelsea still remembered how, during one of the physical challenges, he'd carried her over his shoulder like she weighed nothing, an exhilarating feeling for a tall girl.

Now, though, she felt that torso and those arms for what they were—the body of a sexy, willing, and available man. She'd been flirting with him for weeks, and had been fantasizing about him for almost as long.

"I'm fine," she murmured, pulling back, but not away.

Todd ran his eyes over her face, over her lips, all the way down into the cleavage her dress offered. "Hell yeah, you are."

It was a dumb joke, a totally throwaway line. It was the kind of banter they'd been exchanging all season long, mostly for the cameras, but later for each other. Chelsea should have rolled her eyes. On the show, she had.

But the cameras were gone. They were alone. No one was around. No one would ever know.

She wasn't sure who started it, but the next thing she knew, they were kissing. Like all of the castaways, he'd cut weight over the last month, but his core was still strong. He was still a man's man in a way that she never thought that she'd be so turned on by.

But holy shit, was she *turned on*. Her hands were all over him. Now that she'd started, she couldn't stop touching his bare chest. He was hairless there—another thing that she found hot despite never really giving it much thought—hairless and so chiseled.

In the back of her head, she knew that this was so, *so* wrong. But the ever-present cameras were gone. The pressure was finally off. And flashes of that orgy were still strobing through her brain.

Her dress hit the floor as they entered his room, leaving her in her bra and thong. The bed was there, a little unkempt and oh so tempting, but she turned them to the loveseat instead. The loveseat was safer; so she told herself.

Todd was wearing swimming trunks, she finally noticed. Not the ratty ones from the show, but a newer, cleaner pair that sat low on his hips. Beneath, she saw his erection bulging. Again, she couldn't stop herself. Before she came to her senses, she slid a hand beneath his waistband and touched his cock. She loved how he groaned. She loved how thick he felt. She loved that she turned on this total stud.

He popped her bra off easily and dropped his head down to her nipples. They were hard and swollen, a sign that Todd took as an invitation. As his mouth touched down on her, she nearly came. It had been so long. She needed this.

Todd's free hand slipped into her thong, skimming along her smooth mound. Every nerve ending was bared to him. The fat pads of his fingertips felt so good. "Oh, yes!" she cried. He pressed two fingers into her, and she twisted and writhed on his palm. "Ngh!"

She stroked his dick, jerking him off awkwardly in his swimming shorts as he fingered her. Frustrated, she tugged at the trunks. He got the message, helping her by kicking them off. Like that, she was alone with a naked man who wasn't her husband and who definitely wanted to fuck her.

She needed to get out of there. She knew how wrong this was. She knew that lines were already being crossed. But then Todd leaned in and kissed her again, and his muscled body was there and she silenced that little voice of conscience.

"You're so fucking hot, Chels." He nipped at her ear. "I wanted you as soon as I saw you on that boat."

When he pulled her thong off, she knew what was about to happen. Alarm bells were going off, but still she stroked his dick. This wasn't sex, she told herself. Not technically.

He pressed his body to hers, trapping her hand between them, still wrapped around his cock. He was as bare as she was, either he'd shaved after coming to the resort, or he'd lasered it before the show. Didn't matter. It was intoxicating.

Their kisses grew more heated. He started grinding on her, rubbing that big, hard cock against her tummy. His balls teased her exposed clit.

"Ngh!" she cried, squeezing that throbbing man meat.

Todd ran his hand down her body, along the outside of her thigh. Instinctively, she lifted it, running the inside of her knee in a slow caress along his hip. She felt her body open to him. She felt him shift lower, that thick column of flesh dragging along her sex. She felt every vein, every hard imperfection. She felt the crown of his cockhead catch on her clit. She gasped.

His cock was against her opening, stretching her. She tossed her head back, clutching at his shoulders. He pressed in. She nearly screamed. He felt huge and so good and so different. He was new. He was wrong. This was wrong.

"No," she managed to say. The word came like something squeezed and desperate. "Todd... we can't..."

To his credit, Todd immediately pulled back.

"Right, sorry. Let me grab a condom."

She checked him out as he reached for one of the lacquered boxes that discreetly held the condoms. From his tattoo sleeves to his cut upper body to his large, fully erect cock, he was a specimen of masculinity. He was the guy she never thought she could have, and here he was, ready to give her what would be the fucking of her life. And no one would have to know.

"Todd, I'm... I'm married."

He paused, his hand frozen as he held the square condom foil. She hadn't told anyone in the game about Andy. "What?"

"I'm sorry, I... I led you on." She winced, not sure where this would go. He had every right to be pissed off. "It's all... complicated."

Instead of getting mad, instead of blowing up at her, he took one last look at her naked body, seeing the hottie that Chelsea always tried to hide. She was drop-dead gorgeous, and in the next few months, all of America would see and agree.

After a couple of long breaths, he looked back up in her eyes and grinned and said, "Lucky fucking guy."

Chelsea wanted to laugh, but the guilt stymied that. "I don't know about that. What we just did's not exactly a thing most husbands would want."

"Then it's our secret." He moved close to her and kissed her one last time. She so easily could have just finished the deed. Her pussy ached for that cock again, but no. "Maybe I'll see you around at one of the watch parties."

Some of the cast of past seasons would get together for unofficial watch parties, where they'd watch episodes as a group. She'd seen them on the Instagram accounts of past contestants.

He straightened back up and went to his dresser, rooting out a pair of shorts. Right, this was his room.

She grabbed her dress and pulled it back on. "Maybe," she said.

"If not at one of those, then definitely at the live show, where we crown Jason."

"We're, uh, not supposed to talk about how we vote."

Todd grinned one final time at her. "You're right. We should always follow the rules." He nodded at the door. "I'll go first. You wait here until the coast is clear."

She nodded. He acted like he's done this thing before. Chelsea felt out of her depth. "And Todd?"

"Don't worry. I'll take this to the grave. Goodbye, Chels."

And he was gone.

10

AFTER THE CONFESSION

Chelsea was staring at her now empty glass of wine. There were tears in her eyes. Her nose was red. Andy was right there beside her, his pulse throbbing like the inside of a nightclub, the pressure in his veins so high that he wondered if this was what preceded a heart attack.

"If you want a divorce, I totally understand. I... I'm so *stupid*."

"A divorce?" The idea had never even occurred to Andy, but now that the word was out there, he wondered if that's what she wanted. "Do... do you?"

Chelsea turned to look at him, wiping her eyes, looking confused. "What?"

"Do you want a divorce?" he asked. He'd been waiting for this day since the moment she said 'I do.' Having it arrive like this made it no easier. For all his cuckold leanings, he did not want to lose her, and asking the question felt like a dagger right into his belly.

"No! Me? No." Then she understood where he was coming from. It seemed to click into place for her. "Oh, Andy, this has nothing to do with you. I'm the one who... who... who completely fucked up. You didn't—"

"You deserve someone better than me."

"What does that even mean?"

What did he mean? He'd had the thought countless times, but never had to articulate it to anyone with actual words.

"You're... out of my league. When people see us together, they look at me and wonder how I landed someone like you—"

"First of all, no. Just... *no.*" She emphatically shook her head. "Second of all, you make it sound like I'm some prize to be won. Like all relationships are contests, to the victor go the spoils, and you feel like you've somehow... cheated."

She hesitated at the word, and they both heard the unintended meaning. Shutting her eyes and shaking it off, she soldiered on. "I'm the one who cheated, Andy. I messed up, and I didn't mess up because I think you're not good enough for me, or whatever. You are the best thing to ever happen to me. If anything, *I* don't deserve *you.*" Tears were forming again. "I am so sorry. So, *so* sorry, Andy."

"If it's not about me, then...?"

"It's hard to explain without sounding like I'm making excuses." Henodded, encouraging her to try. She sniffed back her tears and pressed on. "It was probably because you *weren't* there. It was all like... like summer camp. Magical, distant, detached from the rest of the world. And I got caught up in it. And I've been living with that guilt ever since getting back and it's been eating me alive."

Andy pulled her close, holding her against him as she sobbed. The crazy thing was that he didn't feel any anger at her, and the last thing that he wanted to do was lose her. As ironic as it was, for the first time in their relationship, he was starting to realize that she wasn't going anywhere—and it took her nearly fucking another guy to drive that point home.

"I'm not going anywhere," he whispered into her hair. "I love you, Chels. I love you so much."

"We can skip LA. I can call in sick. You know I didn't make it to the final three, so it'll be fine—"

"No, we can't do that." Andy had been anxious about attending the final show, but he'd never considered the possibility of not going. With Chelsea's confession, he knew now that they had to—that he wanted to more than anything. "Pretty sure you've got some contractual obligation."

"Oh, fuck that." It was a very un-Chelsealike thing to say, and she seemed to realize it as soon as she said it, covering her mouth. "You're more important than any of it. You."

"Then we should go." He squeezed her hand. "I'll be there."

She looked at him skeptically.

"Seriously, Chels." Andy was already thinking about watching her and Todd and witnessing all that sexual tension between them in person. Knowing what he knew now, that he'd kissed her, that he'd felt her, that he'd seen her naked, made him so hard. "I've always had this fantasy…"

Shock rolled through as he realized what he was about to say. This was about as out-of-body as it got, yet now that it was coming out, he couldn't stop himself. "I've always had this fantasy of you with another man."

Saying those words out loud was a huge weight off his shoulders.

"Oh, Andy, you don't have to… I'm the one who messed up—"

"It's not a reaction to that. This started long before Todd. I don't know when, and… and I don't really, like, totally understand it, but… yea," he finished lamely.

Chelsea was quiet for a long time, processing it all.

"Please say something, honey," he said, worried now that he'd really fucked up. "I shouldn't have… you know what? Just forget about it—"

Something dawned across Chelsea's face. "You have a fantasy of me being a hotwife."

The fact that Chelsea knew that term floored Andy. His mouth literally fell open.

"That's what it's called, right? A hotwife fantasy?"

"You've... heard about that?" In all the fiction that he'd consumed, all the stories that he'd read and short films that he'd watched, it was always the husbands educating the wives.

"Yeah. That producer I talked with on the show, Camila, told me about the fantasy. She's dated guys who have it, and I guess like to hear about any hookups while traveling. And she's interviewed a few contestants who've mentioned it."

"That..." He didn't know what to say. "Really?"

"She thought that's maybe what you were trying to tell me when you said I was single on the show."

Andy colored.

"Were you?"

"I don't... well, maybe?"

"I didn't believe her," Chelsea hastened to add. "And I'm not using it as an excuse about what happened with Todd."

"But maybe it was there, subconsciously?"

"No." She was clear on this. "No, not even subconsciously. I'd never presume. I'll own my mistake."

"Look, I've never been honest about how I feel, even with myself. At first, I was scared that it would just happen. That you'd wake up and realize that you could have so much more." He held up his hand as she began to protest again. "But later, the thought started to turn me on. Thinking of you with other guys, getting all that pleasure that I can't always give you..." He shivered.

Chelsea squeezed his leg. "You give me so much pleasure, honey."

"I know, but..." He ran his hands along her body.

"I don't need anyone else but you," she said.

"I know." He did, and as he said it aloud, he realized just how profoundly he knew it now. "But this isn't about need. It's about desire."

She was processing it all. It would take time, and he could give that to her. He owed her that much. He'd had years to wrap his head around it. She'd had only a few minutes.

"And right now," he said, taking her hand, "what I desire is to take you upstairs and make love to you."

***

Could it be classified as 'reclamation sex' if it happened three and a half months after her encounter with another man—and that her encounter wasn't full sex? Did it matter? Not really, Andy thought, as he dragged Chelsea up to their bedroom.

Chelsea wore cheerleader shorts and a casual blouse that offered a nice view of her cleavage. Andy imagined her the way Todd had, and was all over her. When Andy kissed her, there was as much pent-up need in her as there was in him. They discarded their clothing. They found the bed.

"I love thongs," Andy groaned. She had an amazing ass, full, ripe, and perfect for the sexy underwear. Todd had seen her in that, too, and it was no wonder that he couldn't contain himself. "You're so sexy, Chelsea."

They were on the bed, kissing. Andy loomed over her as he pressed his hand against the lacy gusset of her panties. She was wet, despite the guilt she was feeling. Her story had excited her, and that realization excited Andy. He wanted to probe more. He wanted to ask her about how big Todd was, how good it felt when he entered her. But now wasn't the time.

Together they kicked off her thong. Andy felt the desperation, once again recalling her story. When she guided his dick to her open legs, he did what Todd had done—he didn't enter her right away. Instead, he teased the crown of his cock along her slippery mound. She was so smooth, so soft—and another man had felt that, too. She'd let it happen. She'd almost let it *all* happen.

"Uhhh!" she groaned as Andy finally sank into her.

Andy almost lost it. Her confession was the realization that he wasn't crazy, that he wasn't paranoid—and that he really did love the idea of her with someone else. He didn't want her last day at Rescue to be the end of her story with Todd. He wanted her to have the full and amazing experience.

"Oh, Andy, you feel so good," Chelsea moaned.

And so hard, he thought. And so powerfully turned on. "You're a... amazing," he groaned, having to slow his hips down and make love to her. Any faster and he'd lose it. They'd had a lot of sex since she returned from filming, but this felt different.

He pressed himself over her, wanting to feel her breasts against his chest and feel her heartbeat. He didn't fuck her. This wasn't that kind of balls-deep rutting—the kind that Todd probably wanted to give Chelsea back in that room.

No, as he reconnected with his wife after her profound confession, all he wanted to do was hold her, to be with her, to make love to her. The fucking would come. The hard sex was for later. In the aftermath of her story, he needed to reclaim her love first, and to demonstrate that Andy was still Andy.

"I love you, Chels," he grunted, close. She put a hand on his ass, pulling him into her.

"I need you," she sighed. Then she repeated it with more urgency. "I *need* you."

He drove faster, but with the same tenderness as before. He pulled back, just enough to look down at her, to nuzzle her nose with his, to kiss her as she breathed and gasped. She was on the cusp. So was he.

"Oh, Chels," he grunted. He shut his eyes and saw her with Todd again, in Todd's room, naked, kissing wildly, groping. He imagined the other man's dick, bare and thick and in his wife's hand, in his wife's pussy. "Oh, Chelsea!"

He came with one last thrust. Chelsea threw her head back, clenched her jaw, and joined him a moment later, sinking her nails into his ass.

Satisfied, they fell together, still as one. They lay together, as one, unburdened by the weight of their secrets for the first time since she'd come home—and for Andy, for so much longer. The conversation wasn't over. There was still so much more to come, but right there, right in bed, at the tail end of their ragged evening, he fell into a deep, restful sleep.

11

DOUBT

"I can't go," Chelsea announced as she walked into the house. She was just back from Pilates, wearing tight black leggings and a sports top that left her abs distractingly bare. "I should have never gone on that stupid show."

"What happened?"

"My instructor hit on me." She sounded more agitated than embarrassed. Andy appreciated the tone, even as a twinge excitement rippled through him.

"What's that have to do with the show?"

"Apparently he watched. He told me that he was really sorry that I was eliminated. Then he asked if I wanted to grab a drink with him sometime."

That twinge of excitement grew inside of Andy. "I mean, the show is pretty popular. I'm sure he's not the only one to recognize you, and you made it far."

"He thought I was single. Available. Despite wearing this." She held up her left hand, as if to prove to him that she still wore the wedding band.

"Some guys don't really see that as a problem."

"Right, no thanks to watching me flirt with guys on network television."

Andy felt his palms begin to sweat and the heat begin to rise on the back of his neck and his cock begin to grow. "So what did you tell him? Your instructor?"

"What? I turned him down, of course. Told him I was taken."

"And how did he react?"

"Embarrassed and apologetic. See, that's the problem—"

"It's not a problem." Andy stepped up and collected his frazzled wife in his arms. "Not for me, anyway."

"Hm? What?"

"Just... I was serious about what I said the other day."

She blushed. "The hotwife thing."

"We should actually talk about that," he said. "But first, you want a drink? I want a drink."

"Um, yes. Yes, that sounds good."

He turned and headed for the kitchen, happy to feel Chelsea just behind him, rather than fleeing out the door, or worse, just standing there speechless. He grabbed the bottle of Maker's Mark from the upper cabinet and two glasses. Chelsea retrieved a couple large ice cubes from the freezer as he poured.

"To finally coming clean about things?" Andy offered in toast.

"To the truth." Chelsea looked nervous as she tapped her glass to his. They both gulped down the entire first pour.

"So your fantasy..."

"I know it's weird."

"No, it's not weird at all. Like you said the other night, it's about desire. I'm sorry, I'm just still processing it all."

Andy refilled as Chelsea studied him.

He ran his hands along her body. Her sweat had cooled on her exposed skin, and when he kissed the spot behind her ear, she tasted salty.

"I've been thinking a lot," he managed to say. "About that night. About Rescue and Todd."

He heard Chelsea's breath catch, but she didn't pull away. They were both into this. "And when you think about it, how does it make you feel?"

"See for yourself." Andy guided her hand down between his legs.

"You're so hard." She stepped closer. "Tell me, what do you think about, with me and Todd? What gets you going the most?"

"Just... the idea of you losing yourself in his arms. Of you kissing, touching, stripping one another."

She squeezed him harder. "What else?" she whispered.

"Tell me honestly, was Todd bigger than me?"

"Andy..."

He lifted her up onto the counter. She went with a yelp. Grasping her leggings, he peeled them down, noting the workout thong she wore. Noting that she was wet with excitement.

"It's okay, Chels. You can tell me." He opened her legs, jerked her thong aside, and buried his face between her thighs, lapping along her smooth gash.

"Ha!" she gasped. "I should... ahhh... take a shower..."

He didn't relent, and she didn't push him away. One thing he was good at, and it was eating pussy. But he also needed answers. The smell of her, mixed with the booze and all this heady talk, had consumed him. "Was he, Chelsea? Tell me. Please."

"Yes!" she groaned. He wasn't sure if that was a cry of pleasure, or an answer. When she clarified, he almost came. "Yes, he was bigger."

Andy pushed his fingers into her as she admitted it and zeroed in on her clit with this tongue. She tossed her head, moaning as she leaned back on the counter.

"And that was exciting," he said between licks.

"Mmm..."

"Different," he pressed, just before pressing a third finger into her pussy. She was tight, but accepted it with a loud cry. Thinking about Todd's cock, about how he'd felt just before she'd told him to stop?

"Yes! He felt... he felt... so different..."

"And it turned you on."

"Uhh, Andy!"

He wanted an answer, but she was already gone, her orgasm overwhelming her. Her thighs squeezed around his face, trapping him as she worked her hips up against his mouth. He rode the storm, working her pussy, imagining her imagining Todd.

Chelsea shuddered when she finally released him. "So good..."

He stood, kissing her abdomen, her ribs, the hem of her exercise top. As he tugged that off, Chelsea recovered enough to reach down and rub his erection through his pants.

"You're so hard."

"Thinking about you and Todd."

She listened, seeming as if she was finally starting to believe.

"I get so hard every time I think about the two of you kissing." Andy kissed her, and she kissed him right back, despite tasting herself on his lips. "I get so hard thinking about how you touched his dick."

Chelsea unzipped Andy's pants and pulled him out.

"You almost fucked him," he breathed.

"Yes." The apologetic tone was gone. "I almost fucked him."

The counter was a good height for oral sex, but terrible for fucking, and the bedroom was just too far away. Andy glanced towards the living room, to the sofa. He couldn't wait even that long, and neither could Chelsea.

He pulled her to the floor, laying on his back on the hard-wood flooring as Chelsea straddled him. She lined him up, needing to feel him as much as he needed her.

"Ah!" she cried as he pushed into her. He stared up at this vision of a woman, all those curves rising above him, tawny and voluptuous.

"Andy... Andy, fuck me!"

He fucked. He held her hips, guiding her bounces, thrusting up to meet her. "You almost fucked him," he gasped. He couldn't let it go, and Chelsea finally seemed to accept it. "And that is so fucking hot, baby."

"Uhh!" She played with her nipples, eyes shut. Imagining him? Andy played with her pussy as she rode him, rubbing her clit with his thumb, his other fingers braced against her smooth, hairless mound.

"Imagine if you hadn't stopped him, Chels," he said. She only rocked her hips harder. "Imagine if you knew that you could do whatever..." Andy's own breath caught. "You... wanted... with him."

"Oh, uhhh!" She was there, grinding her hips into his, her pussy taking every inch of his cock. But she also wasn't there. She was with Todd. She was imagining a much bigger dick, being with a much different man.

Andy joined Chelsea, unable and unwilling to hold back any longer. He caressed her hips, holding her steady as he flexed his core and pumped his come into her warmth.

Chelsea folded herself on top of him, sighing happily. She seemed to recognize their surroundings for the first time. "Did we....? Did we just have sex on the kitchen floor?"

"We did. Like a couple of horny newlyweds."

Chelsea giggled. "Pretty sure we never had sex on the kitchen floor. Like ever."

"And that's a shame." Andy rolled her into her side, so that her skin touched the floor. She shrieked as he said, "Who needs a mattress when you've got cold hardwood like this."

"I think I see some old lettuce over there." She was looking along the baseboard, beneath the counters. "It really is romantic down here."

They shared a final laugh before things inevitably got serious. But the kitchen floor wasn't a place to talk about any of that.

"Come on," Chelsea said, starting to rise. "Take a shower with me. That's something we've never done, either."

———

"Are you *sure* about this?" Chelsea asked.

"I'm sure. But only if you want to."

Their bags were open on our bed. Andy's was completely packed, but his wardrobe was easier. Chelsea had a lot more, from makeup to dresses to lingerie. He got a secret thrill as he watched her fold up some thongs and move them into a packing cube.

She paused, turning to him. "It's not just about what *I* want. It needs to be what *we* want."

Andy moved over to her. They'd been over this again and again over the last few days. Asking and reaffirming. Checking in. Building trust.

"You won't get jealous?" she asked.

"I can't say that I won't. But if it becomes a problem, I'll tell you."

She bit her lip. This felt like those moments just before leaving for Castaway, months ago. Only this time, the adventure that awaited was one they could share. "And if I can't do it?"

Andy kissed her gently. "That's okay, too."

"We can still bail," she said. "Contestants have skipped the live show before."

"You're just nervous to see him again?"

"Well, I mean, yeah." She released a nervous laugh. "There's a reason I didn't go to any watch parties."

"I'll be there. We'll be fine." He reached into her suitcase and withdrew a lacy bra. "We'll definitely be fine."

12

LOS ANGELES

The flight to LA was both long and short. They arrived the morning of the live show, only for Chelsea to quickly leave Andy on his own as she met with the studio's production crew to get her ready.

"You'll be okay?" she asked for the millionth time.

"I'll be fine," Andy said, kissing her. "Don't worry about me. I've never been to LA. Maybe I'll go check out Hollywood."

Andy didn't see her until the afternoon, when he came home to find her in the shower. They'd abstained from doing more than kissing since his confession that he wanted her to fuck Todd. They still hadn't revisited that talk, but it lingered there like an electric current, thrumming in the background, ever present.

Seeing her in the shower, soap suds rolling down her curves and through her cleavage, was a reminder of what could happen later tonight.

He couldn't resist. He joined her in the shower, his dick already hard, his mind already filled with naughty thoughts. "Hey, how's your day been?" Andy asked.

"Just got better, now that you're here."

It still felt amazing kissing her, pulling her warm, soft body to his, feeling her full tits on his chest. She was still soapy, easy to caress, easy to rub. He shuddered as she wrapped a hand around his cock, transferring that soap to his member as she jerked him off.

"You see him?" Andy asked. There was no doubt who 'him' was here.

"Yeah." She stared up at him. "Everyone was there."

"Was it weird?"

"Actually, not even a little. It was more like seeing a good friend after a long time." She bit her lip, realizing what she was implying. "That okay?"

"That's perfect." He pushed his hand down between her thighs, fingering her smooth folds. "Anything happen?"

Chelsea started to laugh, but it ended up a moan. "No. Nothing... happened... we just... talked..." She opened her eyes, focusing on him now. "But he told me that... he missed me... at the watch parties I never went to."

"Now I understand why you turned them all down," Andy said, putting it together. "You wouldn't have been able to control yourself."

Now she did laugh. "I was feeling guilty," she corrected.

Andy pulled his hand away, and Chelsea moaned in protest. "Now you don't need to feel guilty," he said. He kissed her again. "Now you can enjoy it."

"You're really going to leave me in this state?" she asked, turning to him as he started to get out of the shower.

He looked at her full-frontal nudity—all the curves, all the tanned flesh. His cock jumped. He wanted more than anything to go to her, press her up against the shower wall, and fuck her. But they'd made it this far. A little more denial would get them through tonight.

"You don't get to come yet," he said. "The next time you come, you'll be with Todd."

———

THE FINAL EPISODE of the season—episode 13—was broadcast before a live studio audience. At the end, all of the contestants would gather on the stage and Molly Reynolds would announce the winner. It was tradition.

The final episode was the network's opportunity to showcase all of their story arcs they'd edited through the previous 12 episodes and any growth that may have happened, done almost primarily through recaps and slick highlight reels.

This particular finale was kind of anticlimactic, mostly because everyone figured that Jason had won. The show tried to add some kind of drama, playing up the deeds of the other two contestants, but no one was buying it.

It began at 8 pm, which felt late by Philadelphia standards, but Chelsea had to head to makeup and wardrobe hours before then, leaving Andy once again on his own for dinner. Still, the time passed quickly and before he knew it, he was seated in the studio auditorium with a bunch of strangers, watching the end of one of his favorite shows.

It was so surreal. At times, he almost forgot that his wife played such a pivotal part, only for her to show up in a montage as one of the big threats that the three finalists had vanquished. Then came the inevitable announcement that Jason was the winner, and the show transitioned to an entirely live show, which more closely resembled a talk show.

"What was the hardest part of your time on the island?" Molly Reynolds asked. This was several commercial breaks in and getting close to the end of the evening. She had already prodded out some fun confessions from the other cast members. Now she turned back to Chelsea. "Chelsea, let's start with you."

Before answering, Chelsea seemed to look out into the crowd, blinded by the lights. She was looking for him, and Andy did his best to smile and stay calm, knowing that another camera was probably trained on him. He buried the queasy sensation that had been riding him for months now.

Chelsea turned back to Molly and answered. "Definitely being away from home. Missing my support network." She looked at the rest of the contestants. "You all don't know this, but I'm actually married. Eight years last October."

"You never told anyone," Molly stated, unfazed. She must have known. "Why not share that?"

"I never said that I wasn't, either," Chelsea pointed out, blushing. "But yeah, it was deliberate. We talked about it." She looked out towards where she thought Andy sat, growing so red that she eventually covered her face with her hands and laughed nervously.

Molly was relentless, dragging out the confession, just as she did week after week on the show. "What am I seeing here?" the host asked.

"I'm really not this kind of person, Molly, I swear." When she pulled her hands away, she was more composed. "But we just thought... guys would be more open to working with me if they thought they had a chance."

Molly gave her an easy out. "Hey, girl, don't be embarrassed. Use what you've got. Your sexuality is just as potent a tool as your ability to climb a tree or solve a puzzle."

It was hard not to imagine what Chelsea saw—this same host, naked and having group sex with some of the other Castaways.

Jason, the flirtatious winner, didn't help when he added, "Listen to Molly. She definitely knows what she's talking about."

"Oh, you," Molly said, smiling as she waved her hand at the man. "Jason here is the real pro. He had all of you wrapped around his finger."

There was definitely something between those two. Andy saw it, and wondered again if anything had happened. He'd been doing a lot of that kind of wondering.

"Okay, I think it's time to take one last break," Molly said, looking at the camera. "When we get back, we'll get a preview of season 26, then say goodbye to these Castaways."

AFTER THE LIVE SHOW WRAPPED, Andy finally got up on stage to reunite with Chelsea. She was talking with Kim, a petite redhead who was one of her first allies on the show. When she was "cast away" early, it forced Chelsea to change tactics, starting to work with Todd.

This close to Chelsea, Andy could see all the makeup that the network had applied for the cameras. When he gave her a friendly kiss hello, careful not to smudge her lipstick, it felt... awkward. "Hey," he whispered, painfully aware of Kim standing there, probably thinking, *So this is the husband.*

The nervousness that Chelsea had carried with her through the past 12 episodes was back. That had been fine in the privacy of their house, but here, in front of another contestant, it was embarrassing. He didn't want to deal with it, so he looked around and said, "This is all so surreal."

It wasn't a lie. He looked out into the auditorium, the vastness of the seating now emptying as people filtered out. It was huge, and Chelsea had been near the center of it all.

"Yeah," Chelsea agreed.

"I don't know if I could have gotten on stage and talked in

front of all these people." What he was really saying was, *I don't know how the old Chelsea handled it all.*

Kim answered for them. "Well, we couldn't see anyone. Lights were fucking bright as hell. But we were also among friends, as weird as it sounds." She put her arms around Chelsea, who was so much taller. "We only hung out for, like, what? A week? But goddamn, I feel closer to you than most of my sorority sisters."

Kim had been a chatty player on the show, a boisterous source of entertainment. Her personality was as different from Chelsea's as their sizes, which made them a fun pair. As she chattered away, though, Chelsea studied Andy. He felt her eyes, felt her empathetic concern. He gave her a reassuring nod before turning to study the stage instead.

They'd set the stage like they were back on the island. There were fake palm trees around, a tiki theme that gave off a mildly distasteful feeling of appropriation. The torches burning around the set, Andy noticed, were fake. In fact, that was his general takeaway—it was all fake. The show, too, he realized.

He stepped up to Chelsea and took her into his arms. In her heels, she was practically eye level with him. Those eyes sparkled now with eyeshadow and liner, glowing soft brown and ever-concerned.

"I'm good, Chelsea," he whispered. They'd talked about this. He'd reassured her every moment he could in the days leading up to this reunion, but she still never fully believed him. They'd made the decision together that she'd reveal her secret on live national television.

Before Chelsea could respond, though, Kim interjected. "You've got a great guy here, Chels." She had a wide smile, exactly the same as the woman I'd watched on the show. Maybe it wasn't so fake, after all.

"Oh, I know I do," Chelsea said, squeezing him harder.

Andy flushed, taking a look around the stage once again. Most of the Castaways were still up here, chatting with one another—and various family members and partners. They all seemed to like one another.

Jason, the winner, sauntered over to them. Andy could practically feel this man's charisma. He was a stocky guy, not traditionally good looking, but he more than made up for it in presence. He'd grown a mustache since the show had been filmed, and it somehow worked for him. Everything seemed to work for this gregarious guy.

"So you're Chelsea's man," he said, sticking his hand out to Andy. "I knew she had secrets, but this one's a doozy. Nice to meet you."

Andy took it, although Chelsea never stepped away. "You're not hitting on my husband now, too, are you?" she joked.

"I would never," Jason said. "I only save it for the ladies."

Kim snorted. "Or the guys with the 'ladies' you're trying to hit on."

Jason grinned, not denying it. "You're all going to the post-show party, right?"

"Of course," Kim said.

For Chelsea and Andy, the question carried a lot more unintended weight. Todd would be there—Todd, and all the possibilities that came with him. "We'll be there, too," Andy answered for them both. "Wouldn't miss it."

"Wonderful," Jason said. "How long's everyone staying in LA?"

"We're staying through the weekend," Andy said. "Figured if we were taking off work to travel in the middle of the week, might as well make a vacation of it."

"Same!" Kim said. She batted her lashes and added, "I think LA agrees with me, too. Love this weather."

Chelsea laughed. "I couldn't agree more."

"I'm throwing a party tomorrow," Jason said.

"To celebrate you," Chelsea shot back. She wasn't usually this snarky, although she delivered it with a smile, as if chiding a younger brother. "How perfect."

Jason let it roll off him. "To *thank* you for voting for me, yes. It's at a bar in Santa Monica. You should all come."

Someone from the studio came over and instructed them that things were moving back to the hotel, where everyone was staying. Castaway members were being taken separately, so Andy and Chelsea said their goodbyes yet again. Before she could ask him one final time, Andy repeated his mantra, "I'm good, sweetheart. Stop worrying about me, and have fun with your friends."

"I love you, Baby."

He kissed her forehead. "Love you, too." And boy, did he mean it.

Kim sighed. "Now I see why you kept him secret."

Andy watched Chelsea go, surrounded by all those one-time strangers whose video introductions he'd once watched. Andy was shuffled onto a charter bus with actual strangers.

***

"I can't believe the librarian's married," a guy on the bus said, sitting just behind Andy.

Another guy, also behind him, added, "She definitely didn't act like it on the show."

"My brother says that she and Todd were even tighter than what you saw on the show. Said that they only aired a small portion of the time those two spent with each other, towards the end."

"Yeah, that's what I figured. Either she's one really good

fucking actress, or her husband's got a big problem on his hands."

"I bet they did it that last night before the vote. Her bent over a palm tree, the moon behind them, as he drilled her."

The guys laughed. Even knowing it wasn't true, Andy felt a mixture of humiliation and excitement.

"Who's your brother?" the second guy asked.

"Jason!"

"Oh, sweet. You going to see a cut of those winnings?" And the two left the subject of 'the librarian,' moving on to what they'd do if they were suddenly millionaires. Still, the first bit landed pretty hard on Andy.

"You're the husband, aren't you?" the quiet voice of the woman sitting at his side said.

His quick look gave her his answer.

"I thought so." She wasn't accusatory, more like a therapist confirming something. "You okay?"

"I told her to... act single." He'd not actually said that to anyone except Chelsea. It felt pretty good to get off his chest. They didn't have many friends as a couple, and none of the people at his work watched the show.

To his surprise, the woman said, "I know."

"What?"

He looked at her now. She was cute—dark hair, nose stud, nerd-girl glasses, slight Puerto Rican accent. "I'm Camila, a producer on the show. I was assigned to Chelsea. You know all the interviews and confessionals that happen on the beach? I'm one of the people asking the questions."

Andy recognized the name, saying, "Oh, so *you're* Camila. Chelsea talked about you."

"Good things, I hope?"

"Very good," he said. "She liked you a lot."

"That's kind of my deal," she said, adjusting her glasses.

"Well, that and being a release valve. Sometimes the contestants need to just talk, free from the cameras, you know?"

"Well, thank you for that. From both of us."

She smiled. "My pleasure. I love my job sometimes. Nice to put a face to a name, too. She talked about you all the time."

Andy felt kind of embarrassed.

She leaned in and added, "Don't worry about what those guys said. They don't know anything."

Andy only flushed more, seeking to change the subject. "So you get to spend several months out of the year living in the Caribbean. That's pretty nice."

Camila studied him for a moment before letting the subject go. She nodded. "I can't complain. Although one thing I'll say is that it's hard to have a social life outside of work. With two seasons shot every year, we're out there about four to five months. What guy would want to start something with me?"

"I'm sure you wouldn't have that much trouble." As soon as he said it, he felt embarrassed.

Camila just laughed. "You sound just like Chelsea. You two are too kind."

"So you two talked?"

"We did. She's a great woman, and it sounds like you're a great guy. Not many husbands would be able to let their wives have that much freedom."

Phrased like that her statement put all kinds of pressure on Andy—in his gut, his chest, his pants. And like that, they were back on Chelsea.

Camila said, "You really told her to be like Felicity from season 12? You know that's really not her personality?"

"I know, but I didn't want her to hold anything back," he said. "And it seems like she did a pretty good job, unless that was all editing."

"Some of it was, but she did surprise all of us in production.

We don't like to play favorites, but a few of us were rooting for her. She's such a badass."

"Wasn't always like that," Andy said.

"I know! I did the first interviews with her. She was like a country mouse. It was so cute. You know what's funny though? She kind of set the tone for the whole season. Season of the Showmance, some of us were calling it. It was like, when the others saw this unassuming librarian introvert flirting, it gave everyone permission. Usually, that kind of behavior is a red flag and gets you cast away as a threat. With Chelsea, they all kind of coupled up."

"Yeah." Andy didn't know what to say to that.

"But she was never like Felicity. Not really. She didn't have a cutthroat nature."

"So it really was hard to cast Todd off?"

Camila seemed to realize that she'd said too much, her eyes going wide behind her glasses.

Andy sought to reassure her. "It's okay, really."

Camila hesitated before saying, "She was really upset about it afterwards, and before, she was so torn."

Jealousy pulsated through him. "I remember watching that episode," he said. "It was well done, from a production perspective."

Camila winced. "Hard to watch?"

Andy lowered his voice. "Can I be honest?"

"Of course," she said. "I'm used to it."

He went ahead and confessed before he could fully think it through. "It was one of the hottest things I've ever seen."

Camila lifted her eyebrows and pushed her glasses further up the bridge of her nose.

"I mean, it was also tough," he quickly added. "Having her by my side when we were watching made it easier, but..." God, why did he confess that it was hot. His face burned. "I'm sorry, I don't know what I'm talking about."

"It's okay, Andy. I get it."

"You do?"

"You're not the only guy who's felt that way about their partner. You'd be surprised at how many contestants have come into the game with a partner back home who's... open-minded."

Andy sighed. "Less open-minded, more fatalistic."

"Explain that." She sounded like Molly Reynolds, or like the producer that she was, used to interviewing contestants.

"I don't want to lose her," he murmured. "I used to be scared shitless about that." Something about Camila and the way she looked at him, those dark eyes so full of empathy, made him open up in a way that he'd never been able to before. It felt great. "I'd worry that one day, she'd wake up, look at me, look at herself, and realize she could do so much better."

Camila heard the shift in tense. "Used to? But not anymore?"

"I guess this show changed both of us."

"Or maybe," she said, "it's just unlocked something that's always been there."

The bus pulled up to the hotel. People started filtering out. Camila reached over and squeezed his hand. "It was nice to meet you, Andy. You're a great guy, and now I'm even more jealous of Chelsea."

13

THE AFTER PARTY

"**I** feel like I say this at every single one of these, but I think Season 25 has been the best season we've ever done." There was no stage for Molly Reynolds to stand on, but the host made due, standing in a small clearing amidst the gathered crowd.

The post-show party was held on the top floor of the same hotel that most of the out-of-towners were staying in. Made it convenient for those with families to slip away before it got too late, and for everyone else to drink without having to worry about driving home.

"You all made this possible, the sixteen wonderful contestants, yes, but also the rest of you for sharing all that time away from you." Molly folded her hands together and held them to her bosom. "I know it's never easy to be apart from one another, so truly, from the bottom of my heart, thank you." She gestured to the winner, Jason, at her side. "And once again, congratulations, Jason!"

Applause rang through the luxurious reception space.

"Now, enjoy, everyone. No one's going to cast away anyone.

Stay as long as you like. Eat and drink as much as you want. Relax. Have fun!"

The crowd around her dispersed. Andy looked around, seeking Chelsea out. This high up, the large windows gave a spectacular view of the LA sprawl glittering below them. A wide veranda offered outdoor space for people to chill and smoke in the cool, California evening air. He knew this was supposedly only friends and family, but it seemed like there were hundreds of people here.

Chelsea found him first. "Hey, there you are."

"I was just looking for you."

"Sorry. Some of the others wanted to do a Castaway shot." She looked guilty for leaving him alone for so long.

Or maybe guilty for other reasons, a devilish voice whispered. His heart quickened. He pushed it away.

"It's okay, Chels, seriously. I get it. Remember when I dragged you to my high school reunion?"

"Yeah, that was weird. You didn't remember half of your friends' names."

"I was never really close to any of them." He scratched the back of his neck, thinking back to how awkward that was. He really just wanted to go to show Chelsea off to them, a thing that he'd never tell her. "But for me what was really weird about it was the two worlds clashing. I had my high school life and group of 'friends' and then my life with you."

She nodded. "Yeah, this is kind of like that, I guess." He could smell the booze on her breath. It felt rash, underlining the reckless direction that this night could go. He suddenly hoped that it would. Chelsea, thank goodness, couldn't read his mind, and said, "So weird to see everyone all cleaned up."

Andy let her lead the subject away from his forbidden hopes. "I bet this is pretty different from your makeshift shelter on the edge of the beach."

"Yeah." She looked contemplative, as if weighing something. Andy checked her out once again. Her tight bodycon dress was unlike any that she'd ever put on before, selected by the studio, but with no complaints from him. It was so short, and in her heels, her legs looked endless.

"You know, they're all thinking the same thing about you," he said.

Chelsea could still blush at a compliment. That was comforting. "But this isn't really me."

"But it is. At least a part of you, anyway. Just like those dolled up people you see are part of them."

"Mmm hmm."

"And I bet it's fun to get to know more of them, right?" He wanted to call out Todd, specifically, but couldn't find the courage. "If you want to go and keep catching up, I can just..." He looked towards the exit. "I don't mind turning in early."

The thought of leaving her completely alone, with alcohol and Todd and all those reunion vibes flowing, was as irresistible to Andy as a flame is to a moth. But Chelsea wasn't having it.

"You're not leaving me alone, mister." She took his hand. "Come on, let me introduce you." Then, in a callback to his reunion, she added knowingly, "It's my turn to show you off."

What was funny was that Andy already knew all of her Castaway friends, in a sense. He'd watched them weekly. He'd spent more time than even Chelsea knew watching the supplemental videos that the network posted online. They weren't strangers. They were people he'd watched struggle and grow over the last 12 hour-and-a-half long episodes, and here they all were, gathered together like normal people.

He found himself in the company of Kim and Janice, the 44-year-old single mom. She looked fantastic in a strapless tube top and a pair of painted-on white pants. She had a guy with her, who seemed more interested in Rescue, the resort they all went to after being cast off.

"Biggest surprise about Rescue?" the guy asked.

"All the condoms," Janice said with a laugh. "They were everywhere."

"So glad for those!" Kim said.

Janice looked shocked, although Andy was pretty sure it wasn't genuine.

Someone else said, "Didn't you have a girlfriend at home? I thought you were a lesbian."

"Yes, I did have a girlfriend. That didn't last. Also, not a lesbian. The show likes to keep our personas in a neat box, but personally, I like to keep my options open." With a giggle, she added, "and when you get a bunch of sex-deprived twenty and thirty somethings together, there were a lot of options."

"My biggest surprise was how much Molly uses the F bomb," Chelsea said. She seemed eager to change the subject. It worked. Andy looked over at the host, who was currently laughing at something Jason was saying, her hand resting on his arm. She seemed so gregariously friendly.

"Really?" he asked. "I can't imagine her being nasty to anyone."

"Not nasty or mean," Chelsea clarified. "She's not, like, a diva."

Janice picked it up from Chelsea. "She just likes to swear. Like, before we started filming that first scene on the boat, she addressed contestants and crew by saying, *'Alright everyone, we're going to have a great fucking season. Let's get a 'fuck ya!'*"

Kim laughed. "I knew I loved that woman. She's everything you see on TV, only times one thousand."

Andy watched Molly whisper something to Jason before turning back to the group. "So did she and Jason ever...?"

Chelsea said, "I told you, hon, they didn't. She wouldn't sleep with one of the finalists because of ethics."

"Well, she may not have slept with *him*, but there were definitely others..." Kim said.

"No. Who?" someone asked.

"Nope." Kim mimicked zipping her lips closed. "Rumor mill is closed for business. That's for cast only."

Chelsea and Andy exchanged a look. As far as Andy was aware, Chelsea hadn't told Kim about what she'd witnessed, so there must have been more. It was still hard to believe that the host, so professional and put together, did that.

Janice was looking at Molly and Jason flirting and said, "I think it's happening tonight, and with the winner named, it's time to make up for lost time."

"Excuse me, Chelsea," someone said, approaching the group. "Your turn to do your final interview." It was a woman from the network wearing a Castaway polo. "Actually, why don't you two come, too," she said to Janice and Kim. "It's been a nightmare trying to round everyone up."

"One second," Kim said. She stopped a passing caterer, taking two glasses of wine from him and handing them to Chelsea and Janice before taking one of her own. "The *best* interviews come with the right lubrication."

With that, Andy watched the three former competitors be led away. The rest of the group dissipated, leaving Andy awkwardly alone.

Andy found himself in a small group that included Brooklyn and Kyle, the golden couple. If any pairing deserved the name, it was those two with their blond hair and their All-American good looks.

In normal circumstances, he would have been intimidated to even talk to a pair like that. Here, though, with some drinks in him and that uncanny feeling of familiarity he had towards them just from watching the show, he found his voice.

"Congrats on the engagement."

"Thanks." It was clear by the way that they looked at him that they had no idea who he was. No one in this group seemed to. It was a feeling Andy was used to, one that followed him throughout his life. Here, though, he took comfort in that anonymity.

"It's nice to see that some things on the show were real," he said.

"Oh, it was all real," Brooklyn corrected.

"They edited some stuff for dramatic effect, but I didn't see anything on there that didn't seem right."

"What about David and Harry?"

"Definitely real," Kyle said. "Those two were sharing a room at Rescue when I finally got cast away. Although obviously it didn't work out. I think they were just blowing off steam."

"And each other," Brooklyn added.

"For sure."

He didn't have the guts to ask about Chelsea. Someone else, though, didn't have the same hang-up. "What about Todd and Chelsea? They seemed close."

"Oh, they definitely were close." Brooklyn was low-key catty about it, which made sense since Chelsea had orchestrated her elimination, then Kyle's the next week. "Honestly, it was more obvious on the beach than the show made it seem."

"There was plenty of 'cuddling for warmth' happening at night between those two," Kyle added.

Andy lost his voice, his pulse pounding so hard he wondered if this was what a heart attack felt like. He even knew about those little moments. After her confession, Chelsea had filled him in on a few details, although each one felt like pulling a tooth from her.

"Just cuddling?" someone else asked.

"I mean, there are cameras everywhere, and apparently she's married, so yeah, just cuddling," Kyle said.

"And at Rescue?"

Andy held his breath. How much did everyone know? He still wasn't sure. He wasn't sure that he wanted to know... yet he definitely did.

"Honestly, I don't know," Kyle responded. Andy relaxed a little. "They were definitely still flirty."

"Are you kidding me, Kyle?" Brooklyn came back. "I think they definitely hooked up. Did we not watch the same show? If not for all those cameras, those two would have been fucking by day 15, and they were at Rescue for what, four? Five nights? Plenty of time, plenty of opportunity, and there sure as hell was plenty of lust."

"I feel bad for her husband," someone said. "To have to watch that right beside her? I'm surprised he came to this thing."

Andy's face lit up as the others laughed. He laughed right along with them, suddenly wanting to be anywhere but there. Did one of them know that he was actually Chelsea's cuck husband? Were those eyes on him, judging him, thinking him such a pathetic sap?

"Speak of the devils," Brooklyn said, turning her eyes towards the elevators. Chelsea and Todd were walking out, laughing with one another. They looked good like that, like a couple, like lovers.

"Wonder where they're coming from," Kyle said, chuckling.

Brooklyn made a loop with her thumb and forefinger, brought it to her mouth, and mimed giving a blowjob. It was so juvenile, but got right to the heart of Andy's fantasy. God, was it true? The rest of them laughed, especially when Chelsea took a glass of wine from a passing caterer and sipped.

Brooklyn said, "Yeah, wash out the taste of come, you slut, before hubby discovers you."

Andy got out of there. Enough was enough. Time to hide. He didn't head towards Chelsea and Todd, though, aware of all the eyes on the two. Last thing he wanted to do was out himself as the husband to this bunch.

Slinking away, hearing their snarky laughs, it felt like high school all over again. He went somewhere to hide.

He went out to the veranda, needing some fresh air after the stifling crowds and even more stifling conversation. He wondered if this was how Chelsea felt on the show, needing space away from these people. Maybe that was why she so often found herself sitting on the beach, staring at the horizon.

Here, the view to the horizon was filled with LA's sprawl, a grid of lights that ended only at the dark hills beyond. There was a beauty to that, too, an ocean of humanity.

There were people out here, although not as dense as inside. They left him alone, carrying on their conversations. He caught snippets of them. Most were about Jason and how masterfully he won this year, slipping under the radar with his charm until it was too late.

"I liked Chelsea's chances," a woman said. Andy braced himself for some comment about her and Todd, but it never came.

"She was a total badass. They all saw it coming, yet she still made it to the final four."

"If she'd been one second quicker on that last challenge, she would have won."

"One hundred percent."

It was enough to put the wind back into Andy's sails. Ever

since the episode that Chelsea had entered into her secret pact with Todd, Andy had been consumed by it. Everything was framed by that relationship. He filtered out everything else, all other discussion. It was refreshing to realize that most people didn't see it that way.

"Everyone's going on about how great a social game Jason played, but man, I think Chelsea's was better."

Andy kept looking out at the horizon, smiling to himself as he eavesdropped.

"She had all the relationships shored up. She was adaptable. I think the show made a bigger deal out of her and Todd. He wasn't her only ally. You don't make it that far with just one."

Andy nodded, although his nerves were back. Here's where someone speculates on whether the two hooked up, or how surprised they were that she was actually married.

"Jason wouldn't have won if she wasn't playing. People always talk about how the physical guys are the big threats, but Chelsea redefined that."

"Girl power," another said. "That chick changed the game from here on out."

Or not. The women moved on, disappearing back inside. Andy stayed out there, unable to stop smiling to himself. Chelsea was amazing in so many ways, and he was still discovering new surprises. Life was change, and he was happy that he could change with her.

He was still outside on the veranda when Chelsea joined him. The evening air was crisp, and in her little dress, she shivered. "You doing okay?" she asked.

"Yeah." All the overheard conversations, the secret humiliations, his profound excitement were packed into that 'yeah.' Chelsea heard it, too.

"I saw you talking to Brooklyn and Kyle."

"A lovely couple." They laughed at how untrue that was.

"Any fun stories there?"

"They don't know what went down at Rescue between you… two." Still hard for him to say Todd's name. "But they were definitely speculating."

"I'm sorry."

"They didn't know who I was," he said. "So actually, it was really hot to hear."

"I still don't fully understand it."

"But you believe it now?"

Chelsea nodded. "Coming to terms with it."

"I saw you talking with Todd." Andy existed in a semi-permanent state of arousal, but now his pants really started to grow tight. It didn't help to watch his wife blush at that. Then he asked her the question she'd just posed to him. "Any fun stories there?"

"We did a quick interview together. Camila thought it would be cute to show us just as friends."

Andy was getting warm beneath his clothes. "I bet it was cute."

Chelsea stepped closer. "After, on our way out, I took his hand and pulled him into a little meeting room."

Her eyes were locked on Andy's, and there was no hiding from that. She saw everything—his fear, his angst, his excitement. She definitely saw the way he gulped before asking, "Did you?"

"Would you be upset if I did?"

"No," he said. There was barely enough air in his lungs to push that word out.

"And what if I told you that in that little meeting room, I locked the door, got on my knees, and gave Todd a blowjob?"

Andy shuddered, Brooklyn's snarky comment about washing

Todd's come out with champagne coming to mind. It was the closest that he'd ever gotten to coming without any contact.

"Really?"

"No." She was so close he could smell the clean, lavender scent of her shampoo. He could see the mascara they'd applied around her eyes. "But I did kiss him."

In some ways, that landed harder than the idea of a blowjob. It hit hard because he knew it was true.

"I bet he liked that." Their voices low, just loud enough to carry the short distance between them. In the moment, they were alone in all the bustle of the party.

"You like the idea, too," she said.

"Yes."

"He gave me this." Between them, she produced a card, and for a second, Andy didn't know what he was looking at. "What should I do?"

Then it dawned on him. It was a hotel keycard. Todd's hotel keycard.

"I'm okay if you want to go," he said. "And I'll be here when you come back." He studied her, watching her battle desire and propriety in those large and luminous eyes—eyes that had captivated audiences for the last two months.

"Are you sure?" Her question was enough of an answer for him. Andy was suddenly weightless.

"I'm so sure."

She nodded. "I love you, Andy." She wrapped her arms around his neck and squeezed him tightly. "I love you so, so much."

"I love you, too, Chels, and I love what you're about to do." They kissed one another—a goodbye-for-now kiss. "Stay with him as long as you want. I'll be there for you when you're back, and I want to hear all about it."

"God, you're amazing." She kissed him one last time before

stepping away. Andy watched her go, her curves shifting beneath that tight, pale pink dress. He couldn't believe he was letting a woman like that walk away.

Then again, she wasn't leaving. She'd come back to him. He knew that now. She glanced back one last time, smiling at him. Then someone passed between them and she was gone.

14

ALONE BUT NOT

Andy lingered outside, wondering what to do next—both in the immediate term, and all the days to follow. He considered going down to his room, but the thought of just sitting there alone in a strange city sounded depressing, and there was still fun to be had up here.

Inside, he noticed that the party had started to thin out. Anyone who brought their children were long gone, but now a greater contingent had left, too. Those remaining were a fun bunch, though, perfect for people watching.

Chelsea's friend, Kim, was in a small cluster with single-mom Janice, and the young, personal trainer, Isaiah. Andy couldn't look at that grouping and not think about the foursome that Chelsea had discovered, with Isaiah in the middle of Brooklyn and Molly Reynolds.

Speaking of the host, she wasn't there. Neither was the season winner, Jason. Could have been a coincidence, but Jason didn't seem like the type who turned in early for anything—especially not his own celebration.

Normally, after surveying a crowd like this, Andy would quietly slip away, feeling shy. He resisted that urge and went to the bar instead, ordering a club soda with lime. Time to start sobering up.

Camila, the producer and Chelsea's show confidante, was in line in front of him, although he didn't realize it until she turned and looked up at him in her glasses. On the bus, he didn't get the full picture of her. In line, he had plenty of time to admire her lean, modelesque body, sheathed in a pair of wide-flaring white pants and a strapless top.

"Hey, Andy." Even her soft accent sounded more sensual. "You're still here." She glanced around. "And Chelsea isn't."

Andy colored. "No. She… isn't."

He wondered how much she knew versus what she just suspected. If anyone knew the truth, though, it was this woman. She asked, "Are you okay?"

"Is this an interview?"

Camila had a delightful laugh. "The cameras are all off, I promise."

"I'm literally shaking right now." He held up his hand to demonstrate. "I'm scared shitless. Like, I keep thinking, 'What the hell am I doing?' You know?"

"I can imagine." She put a hand on his arm and guided him away from the bartender's station. "You don't have to tell me anything. We can just sit here and gossip about the people around here, if you want. To pass the time."

That sounded nice to Andy, but he couldn't pass up the opportunity to talk to the one person who knew what was going on with Chelsea and him. "It's okay. I don't mind. So you know that she's with Todd right now?"

Those words bubbled up through him like something physical.

"I figured they were, but I didn't know."

Andy nodded. He appreciated Chelsea's discretion, even

with Camila. He said, "We talked. I'm not sure you know, but something almost happened between them at Rescue."

Camila nodded slowly, processing. "I didn't know that either..."

"But you figured?" he asked, repeating her previous answer.

"Things seemed a little awkward between them on the final morning, but I didn't want to assume."

"She confessed. We talked about it. I gave her the green light tonight, if she wanted it."

Camila released a soft puff of air through her pursed lips. "You're a cool dude. She's lucky to have you."

"Am I crazy?"

Camila laughed. "Maybe a little. But don't worry. She loves you, *amigo.* I cannot stress this enough. She talked about you all the time. She worried what you'd think of her when she got home. She worried about how we'd edit her, that she'd be, like, a villain or something."

"If anything, watching that show with her made me appreciate what I have even more," I said.

"Oh, and I should thank you."

"Me?"

"For helping open her eyes to me, I guess. To the whole hotwife fantasy."

"Well, I didn't know you had it. I didn't know you at all. But based on what she was telling me, I had a hunch. Glad I was right. Most guys would freak the F out."

"I think a part of me is still freaking the F out right now."

Camila put a hand on Andy's arm. She had amazing eyes behind those glasses, dark and empathetic. "Anything I can do to help?"

The suggestion was clear. And while that would have been a lot of fun, Andy couldn't do it. Not without talking to his wife first.

"I'm flattered. Like, really flattered, actually. You're really... attractive, and—"

"Hey, no worries, man. I get it. Talk to Chelsea. Maybe we can work out some kind of agreement if you stay longer in LA."

"Stay longer?"

"Todd lives here, and after tonight, knowing him, he won't be satisfied with just a taste."

Andy hadn't considered that, and it felt exciting now that he was. He scratched the back of his neck. "So how about that gossip?"

"What do you want to know?"

"Sounded like things were pretty wild at Rescue. That true?"

"You get a bunch of attractive young people together, unable to access anything from the outside for an extended period of time—including porn—and things get interesting, yes. This season's cast seemed more into it than ever."

Andy wondered what would have happened if Chelsea had been cast away earlier. Would she have been able to hold off, or would she have been sharing a bed with Todd in those remaining days.

"Just the cast?" he probed.

Camila raised a brow. "Are you asking about my own sex life?"

"I may be curious."

"Well, I don't kiss and tell, but there may have been a few that I did kiss..."

"Maybe a hint?"

Kim wandered into their company before she could go on, the redhead glancing between the two of them with a knowing smile. "What's going on here?"

"Andy wants to know if I've ever slept with a contestant."

"Does he now?" She put a hand around Camila's waist and

rested her head on the other woman's shoulder. "And what did you tell him?"

"She wouldn't," Andy answered.

"Discrete," Kim said. "A producer is meant to blend into the background." She turned her head and kissed Camila softly on the neck. "But this one's too fucking hot to totally blend."

Camila blushed, looking shyly at Andy.

"Where's Chelsea?" Kim asked.

"Um... she left with Todd," he said.

"Damn." Kim's grin was wide. "Fuck, that's hot. I take it you're cool with that?"

Camila studied him as he answered. "Yeah, I'm cool."

"Let's invite him back with us," Kim said to Camila. "I want to feel a dick in me as I lick your pussy. Best of both worlds."

Camila raised her brows at Andy, who was more tempted than ever. But she knew his answer. "I offered already. He needs to work it out with his wife, first."

Kim eyed Andy one last time. "Shame. Maybe another day." She slipped her hand into Camila's. "Come on, I'm horny as fuck and am done with this place."

Unlike Todd and Chelsea, the two didn't leave separately, and anyone who watched them go knew exactly what came next.

At last, Andy decided to call it a night, too. He looked one last time around the room, at the dregs of the evening, people clinging to the last of the party as things got sloppy. What a night. He headed for the elevators.

When he got back to his hotel room, it was just before midnight, and Andy half-expected to find Chelsea waiting for him, like it was all a ruse. He was so prepared for it that when he opened the door to a dark and empty room, a shock passed through him.

This was totally different than all the nights during filming, when he'd sleep alone in his bed. As he got ready, there were little reminders everywhere about what was happening, about this next exciting adventure.

Looking into the bathroom, Andy could practically feel her soft curves against him in the shower, beneath his soapy hands. He could almost taste the bubbles that clung to her neck as he kissed her there.

Beside the bed, he remembered their final conversation before she'd left to get ready for the show.

"I can't wait to see what makeup and wardrobe does to you."

"Always trying to doll me up."

"You don't need any of it, and you know it. You attracted Todd in rags and dirt on your face."

"You're going to love my dress. It's short and tight."

"And Todd?"

"I know he'll love it."

Andy finished brushing his teeth and washing his face. He thought of what he'd said to in the shower, after he'd worked her right up to the edge of orgasm. *"You don't get to come yet,"* he'd said. *"The next time you come, you'll be with Todd."*

Out of the bathroom and looking at the bed, he realized just how tired he was. He was jetlagged, and despite switching to club soda, the drinks had finally caught up with him.

He still hadn't heard from Chelsea, but wasn't expecting it. He'd read about husbands in these positions many times, and now he got to feel what they felt. He was restless. He was helpless. He was electrified.

But he didn't panic. He didn't text her, didn't call her, didn't worry. He knew where she was and who she was with. She was safe, and when it was over, she'd be home.

It was surprisingly easy to fall asleep.

15

———

THE WAIT

Andy slept in fits and starts, swimming out of torrid dreams of sex and heartache. He didn't check the clock. He didn't check his phone. He just rolled over and tried to get back to sleep. She'd come back when she was done.

Only when he woke in the morning, she was still not there. It was still early, but the sun was leaking in around the blackout curtains. Andy's heart dropped as he felt the cold space and undisturbed sheets on her side. So maybe it was Castaway filming all over again. Maybe he'd made a grave mistake.

He checked his phone, finally seeing a string of missed texts. Shit. The texts started at 5:15 am.

OMG, I fell asleep! I'm so sorry!

I hope you're sleeping. It's so late. Or so early. Or whatever.

I love you so much, Andy. You are an amazing man, and I am so lucky. And I cannot wait to tell you all about last night. I'll talk to you when you wake up. Right now, I'm going to wake Todd up with a blowjob. The man is a fuck-machine.

Hours later, around 6:30, the texts started again.

Good morning! Hope you get up soon. Could you bring me a

change of clothes to room 1925? Don't really want to do the walk of shame through this hotel.

Don't worry, Todd's down at the gym for now.

That was about an hour ago. I started to type out a response as a new text slid into view.

Actually, he's back now. Text me or call when you're up.

It was actually happening. Right now. Andy squeezed the phone as if squeezing air out of his lungs. Then he snapped out of it and his thumbs went back to work.

[Andy]: Take your time.

To his surprise, he saw the jumping dots as she worked out a response.

[Chelsea]: You're awake!

[Andy]: Just got up. Didn't sleep all that well.

[Chelsea]: Same, but for other reasons.

This was followed by a winky face.

[Andy]: You have fun?

The dots bounced, then stopped, then bounced again. He waited for an essay. Instead, he got a simple, "Yes."

They'd talk about it later. Those dots were no longer bouncing, but his wife probably was. That didn't mean that he was going to just sit in his room, though. He was over that, and now he had a room number.

He took a quick shower to wash away some of the exhaustion of his restless night, threw on some clothes, and filled a small bag with a change of clothing for Chelsea. Fifteen minutes had passed. He wondered if they were still going at it. Without dwelling on it much more than that, he headed for the 19th floor.

Room 1925 was at the very end of the hallway, and as he walked down the hall, it seemed to grow longer and longer, like a nightmare. His blood pressure rose. His pulse throbbed between his ears. His cock was so hard.

He could hear them when he was a full room's length away. Chelsea's cries of ecstasy and another, deeper man's groans. "Oh! Oh! Harder!"

Andy stumbled. As muffled as that was, there was no questioning it. That was his wife in there, begging to be fucked harder.

"Fuck, you feel good!" Todd's voice now. "So fuckin' good!"

Andy drew closer. His grip loosened on the bag of clothing. He slowed with each stop.

"Ngh! God, you feel so big."

Andy gasped.

"You can't get enough of it, can you?"

In response, Chelsea's moans crested in a messy, guttural orgasm. Andy was right at the door now, his ear against the wood, listening to the moans, the heavy breathing, the creak of a bed squeaking under their vigorous sex.

But he couldn't be there for long. It was morning. People were starting to come and go. Directly across from the room was a small alcove that housed the ice machine. He ducked into there, hoping that no one needed to use it.

The sex sounds died down. With his back to the wall, Andy fought to calm his breathing, too. He pulled out his phone, distracted himself there. It didn't take long before Chelsea's text arrived.

Okay, come in five please.

A second later, the door across the hall opened. Todd was humming to himself as he left. Andy peeked around the corner, watching the man stroll down the endless hallway like he was the man of the hour. After what he'd just heard, Andy understood why.

As soon as Todd was out of sight, Andy was knocking at the door. When Chelsea didn't immediately open it, he sent her a text, telling her that he was there.

She opened the door a second later, the sheets pulled up around her body, her shoulders bare. Despite having a long night of fucking, she looked good. Her hair was a little mussed, but when she ran her fingers through it, it still looked as dark and glossy as ever.

"That was quick," she said, glancing down the hall. "Did you pass...?"

"No, I came early. I was..." Andy thrust his thumb over his shoulder, and she followed it to the ice machine alcove. "I... heard."

Chelsea colored. "Sorry about that."

"Don't apologize. I liked it." He stepped inside, right up to her. She smelled like sex. "I *really* liked it."

He shut the door behind him and pulled her into his arms, kissing her hard. She tasted astringent—his come. He was tasting Todd's come.

When they broke the kiss, Chelsea pursed her lips, looking bashful. She knew what he'd just tasted. "I'm sorry, I should have warned you..."

"It's okay." He wasn't going to admit that even that was exciting in its own way. Instead, he looked past her, at the wreck of a room.

Chelsea was wearing most of the sheets off the bed. What remained was tossed all over the place, as were their clothes. The bedspread itself had a few damp spots from where they'd just fucked, and everything smelled of sex.

"This is quite a scene, Chels."

She glanced over her shoulder. An empty platter of food was balanced on the dresser. One high heel lay beside it. The other was on the other side of the room. Condom wrappers seemed to be everywhere.

"I feel bad for housekeeping," she said.

"But not for me?"

She turned to look at Andy, studying him. "I don't think so, no. This room will haunt you for a while, but in a good way." She took the bag from him. "Thanks for bringing me my clothes."

With that, she dropped the sheets around her. Naked, she was somehow both the same as yesterday morning, and entirely transformed. Her nipples looked swollen. Her skin was more flushed. Her pussy puffier. But it was the way she carried the nudity that felt completely new—although maybe that had been growing since the show.

She stepped into the clean thong that he'd brought for her, and when she did, she turned to show off her ass. Her cheeks were red, and there was a clear handprint on one. Her tight jeans quickly took the view away, but it would be forever burned into Andy's retina.

He went to her as she pulled on her bra and hugged her from behind. "You're so sexy, Chelsea."

"Thanks. I feel... trashy, honestly." She pulled her shirt on.

"You are the most precious thing I have ever held."

"Aw." She turned and kissed him quickly. Then she went around the room, gathering her strewn things. "We'll see how you feel after I tell you what I did."

"So tell me."

"Not here." She looked around at the ruins of the room before linking arms with Andy and guiding him out into the hallway. "For story time, we need to do that in our own space."

"Okay."

"But first, I really need you to fuck me."

Andy looked at her as they picked up their pace down the hall. "Really? You're not, like, too sore?"

"Oh, I'm sore. But I don't care. After all, we're a team." They arrived at the elevators. She thumbed the down button. "I need you to make us... *us* again. Okay?"

"I have been holding back since last week," he said. "You have no idea how badly I want you."

"Poor baby. Let me make it all up to you."

By the time they arrived at their room, they were giggling and running down the hall, holding hands and ready for the next big thing.

16

———

LAST NIGHT

"**A**ndy! Yes! Uhh! Yes!"

Andy was on top of her, holding her thighs against his body, pressing his chest to hers. He needed to feel the skin-on-skin contact. He needed to feel as much of his wife as possible as they reconnected.

She felt different, though. Looser. More supple. Like an athlete after a hard workout and a long stretch. But when she moaned, when she gasped, all of that was for him.

They hadn't spoken about last night. Not yet. That story time was yet to come, but there was no doubt—Chelsea was a confirmed hotwife, and he was experiencing his first reclaim. He was gentle with her, making love, gently rolling his hips along her body, savoring the reconnection. It's what they both needed. It was all Chelsea could take.

"You feel so good, Andy," she sighed. She ran her hands over his back, up the nape of his neck and into his hair. She squeezed him tightly, pulling him down to her, like she wanted him all the way inside. "Mmm, baby, yes... yes..."

He flattened his body to hers, kissing her neck and the soft cheek. He ran his hands down her sides and up her legs. He thrust faster, his shallow breaths telegraphing his state.

"Come, Andy. Give me your come."

He took her just a little faster. His balls were so full. He'd been in denial for too long.

"I'll always be here for you, Chelsea."

"Uhhhn... I know..." She squeezed him harder, pulling his head against her shoulder, until they were cheek-to-cheek, as close as they could get. "Now come, baby. I need to feel—OHH!"

Andy was there, falling through the last membrane of willpower. Chelsea had fucked another man. Chelsea had spent the *entire night* fucking another man. She'd fucked him that morning. She was probably thinking about fucking him again.

Yet she was back in Andy's arms. She was asking for him. She wasn't going to leave him or discard him or see him as some lesser man. She was there, beneath him yet somehow in control, and she was asking for his come.

So he gave it.

"Oh, Chels!"

"Andy! Yes!"

And Chelsea was right there with him, flying high on the reclamation, soaring into a whole new hotwife world.

***

After, they got cleaned up. They took a shower together, soaping each other up, kissing, but refraining from more. And refraining from talking about last night until they were both back in bed. Neither of them bothered with clothes, though, preferring to feel their skin on each other.

Side-by-side, legs entwined, with Chelsea softly brushing her fingers through Andy's hair, she began.

"I promised I'd tell you everything, but... you really want to hear everything?"

Andy had been hard since the shower. He stiffened once again at the question. "Everything. Yes."

She nodded. "I thought so." She kissed his forehead. "It's the least I can do after last night."

"Intense?"

She nodded.

Andy said, "But intense in a good way." When she hesitated to answer, he encouraged her with a nod. "It's okay. I want to hear it. The whole, unvarnished truth."

"It was one of the craziest, most intense nights of my life." Her eyes were wide as saucers. "I'm sorry, Andy."

"It's okay. Really."

"Not just because of Todd. I mean, he was... good."

"In bed," Andy clarified.

"Yes. He was good in bed. And on the desk, and in the shower, and on the sink—"

"Okay, okay, I get it." The two laughed.

"But it was also intense because it wasn't you. There was this... wrongness to everything. From even before I got to his room. *'I shouldn't be doing this,'* I kept thinking. Yet..."

"Yet you wanted to."

Chelsea's face burned. "Yes," she whispered. "I'm s—"

"Don't apologize, honey. I get it. It turns me on, too."

She took a deep breath and nodded. "I almost didn't go. I almost came to my senses..."

TWICE, Chelsea almost turned around. Twice, she actually got off the elevator before it reached Todd's floor. She stepped out, feeling overheated and hyperventilating, twisting his keycard again and again in her hands.

It didn't help that the elevator doors in each lobby were mirrored, reflecting back a woman that she barely recognized. She resisted the urge to tug at the short hem on her pink dress, knowing that all it would do was expose more cleavage.

But when they'd selected the dress for her, the first thing that she'd thought wasn't how short it was, or how it looked painted on. It wasn't even about how much her husband would love it. Her very first, very guilty thought, was how Todd would like it. She carried that thought now, along with all that guilt.

"I'm okay if you want to go..." Andy had said, and she felt so ashamed that she *did* want to go. She shouldn't want anyone other than her husband. His answer was to a question that she shouldn't even be having.

But she did want it. And Andy did, too. Camila had been right, he had the fantasy. Maybe deep down, Chelsea knew it, too. She always figured he was just being jealous, and that made her guarded around other men. But Andy wasn't the possessive type. It's what she loved so much about him.

She squeezed the hotel keycard so hard it left an impression in the palm of her hand, then thumbed the elevator button again. Fuck it, all parties knew she wasn't going to turn around. She was just delaying the inevitable.

Arriving at the door, she wasn't sure what the etiquette was. Knock? She had a key. Just go in? She startled when someone down the hall emerged wearing nothing but a hotel robe. He waved at her, and her face bloomed bright red. She swiped the card along the door pad, heard the lock disengage, and rushed inside before she had to deal with the guy.

"You came." Todd was lounging on the bed, reading something on his phone. It was so domestic that Chelsea nearly laughed.

"Looking at porn?" she teased.

"Better. I'm watching myself on the Live Reunion Show."

God, he had such a good, boyish grin. It wasn't fair for him to be so handsome and so arrogant all at once. He tossed his phone down and nearly hopped off the bed, his eyes traveling nakedly over her body.

"You are so fuckin' hot, Chels. Jesus."

This man sure knew how to make her blush. He also helped her out of her shell. "You're not so bad yourself."

She swept her eyes along his body. He still wore the outfit that the studio had chosen for him—a patterned shirt that hung untucked over slim-cut jeans and a pair of boots.

Todd didn't shy away from her appraisal. He didn't blush. Instead, he moved closer to her, and she to him, his hands out before him, palms up. When they were close, he collected her into his arms and pulled her against him.

They'd hugged before, plenty of times—after winning immunity on the show, waking up in the morning after a hard night, surviving a grueling vote and not getting cast away. But this hug was different. This hug was hungry.

"I like the scruff." She touched his face, enjoying the scratch beneath her fingers. It reminded her of the beach. It reminded her of their beginning.

She stared into his eyes—deep blue eyes, like the Caribbean ocean. Then she shifted her focus to his lips. He didn't need any further invitation. He leaned in and like that, they were kissing.

Chelsea felt herself swoon into the kiss, like her feet were floating an inch off the ground. His mouth was so different from Andy's. The way he kissed her was so much more demanding, and in that demand, she found herself wanting to yield.

They made out like teens, growing more frantic, more desperate. Todd pressed her against the wall, kissing down her jawline and the nape of her neck. His hands groped, cupping her tits. Her nipples hardened at his touch. Her pussy grew so wet.

She pushed her hands beneath his shirt, needing to feel his skin, needing to trace his muscles. God, his abs. It felt like he had a million of them.

Todd yanked his shirt off, giving her free access. She took a moment to stare, to admire. The tattoos that she'd gotten so used to on the show were new all over again, the kind of beautiful inked artwork that she'd never appreciated until she saw it etched on this man. His chest was still smooth, like a swimmer's build—if that swimmer was also a punk rocker.

"I like it when you look at me like a slab of meat," he said.

She kissed him hard, her need for him starting to boil over. She maneuvered him around until he was the one against the wall. Her stomach fluttered as she considered what she was about to do. Then she did it, sinking down to her knees.

She worked open his pants, her nails a glossy pale pink to match her dress. How different that was from those days when she had dirt perpetually beneath them. Todd, too, had clean, powerful hands—hands that unzipped his fly, thumbs that hooked into his trousers as he pushed them down his hips.

He wore tight, black boxer-briefs that stretched around his thick cock and even thicker thighs. She ran her hands over those thighs, feeling the power in them. Whenever she looked back on this moment, her first time with another man, she'd think of Todd's muscular thighs. Andy was fit, but this man took things to the next level.

Looking up, Chelsea met Todd's eyes so far above her, watching her, both expectant and excited. She gave her most saucy smile before grasping his underwear and pulling down.

His dick sprang free, just as huge and hard as she remembered. She'd been dreaming about this dick since that night, imagining getting back to that moment, wondering what it would feel like in her hands again, in her mouth.

He was as nicely manscaped as she remembered, too, completely bare, right down to the root. She ran her hands over his shaft, squeezing the supple skin, cupping his heavy balls. "Your balls are so full," she groaned, almost to herself.

"I've been saving myself for you."

"Then let's not keep you waiting any longer." With the flick of her hair, she kept her gaze locked with his as she leaned in and wrapped her lips around his forbidden dick.

Again, she felt guilty for comparing Todd to Andy, but couldn't help it. Todd felt so much bigger in her mouth, his girth filling her as she sucked down, her cheeks squeezing around the cockhead.

She watched his eyes soften as she swirled that dick with her tongue, then swallowed half of the shaft. It felt good to weaken a man like Todd. She may be on her knees, but she was the one in control, setting the pace.

Chelsea didn't have much experience with blowjobs before Andy, and Todd was too big to take all the way. She used her hands to stroke what she couldn't swallow, rubbing his spit into the shaft and caressing his balls. She lost herself in that dick, closing her eyes as she pulled off and licked down the outside. He was so soft. So smooth. Yet underneath it all, such a fucking man. She sucked his balls into her mouth, feeling his knees buckle before he caught himself against the wall, hearing him grunt and curse.

"Damn, girl, that looks so good."

Looks. Not feels. For Todd, it was a show. Andy got like this too, although he never said anything. She fixed her eyes back on him as she wrapped her hand around his dick and started sucking on him again, turning her head so he could see the impression of his cock bulge out the side of her cheek. She swallowed him deeper than ever, relaxing her throat to take the tip.

"Ngh!" she choked, pulling back as she gagged. Even that was sexy for Todd. When she tried again, he widened his stance and tipped her head back against the wall. His breathing grew shallow. He started to pump his hips into her.

He was close.

And she wanted his come.

"Fuck, Chels..."

She watched this sexy, ripped stud start to lose himself above her. She redoubled her efforts, jacking with her right hand, bobbing her head, swirling her tongue, preparing to receive.

Chelsea watched his body seize up, his abs and pecs flex. He rolled his shoulders back, clenched his teeth, and erupted in her mouth. She was ready for it, closing her lips around him as she swallowed this other man's come.

When he was done, she sat back on her heels and smiled up at him, wiping a dollop of semen from her lips like she'd just had a delicious meal. It wasn't, but men like to think that's what they're offering.

"That was..." Todd laughed gruffly. "Fuck, that was hot."

He reached down, wrapped his hand around his dick, and started stroking it back to life. It obeyed. "But I'm ready for more, and you're still in that dress. Damn."

She rose to her feet, rubbing her hand over his balls, over his washboard stomach, over his pecs. She loved tall men. She loved muscles. She couldn't wait to feel this man take her.

And then they were kissing again. He unzipped her dress on their way to the bed, and together they peeled the tight thing off. Her strapless bra matched, the same pale pink as her dress. That, too, hit the floor before they reached the bed, leaving her in nothing but her high heels and pink thong.

"Damn, you're so hot, Chels," Todd said between kisses. His

hands were all over her body, callused and hard, a working man's touch. She loved it, reveling in how new this all felt. She was stroking him again, getting him nice and hard. Getting him ready to fuck her. "Can't take much more teasing, babe."

Chelsea was ready for it. She reached for her purse and removed one of the condoms that Andy had slipped in there for her. That was the moment when she knew Andy was for real. He'd purchased the extra large Trojans. This wasn't a game anymore.

"No more teasing," Chelsea agreed, tearing the condom wrapper open with her teeth. "No more foreplay." She rolled it down his dick. "Time for fucking."

She pulled her thong off, taking a moment to rub her pussy. She was now used to her bald eagle look, but again understood how important presentation was. Todd feasted on her sex as she rubbed her fingers along her bare folds. She mounted him, replacing her fingers with his cockhead.

"Uhhn, you're so hard," she moaned.

The way Todd checked her out—her naked body rising above him—filled her with adrenaline and lust. She lined his dick up with her pussy, shifted her hips forward, and let him open her up.

It was everything she'd been dreaming. It was the harmonic note in a chord that had begun five months ago. He was just as big as she remembered. He filled her every bit, and then *so* much more.

"Ohhh!" she moaned. This wasn't just a taste. This wasn't just the very tip. This was all of him, all eight-plus inches of this new man, sinking all, the, way. "OH YES!"

Pleasure rippled through her. Was that an orgasm? Did she just come? If so, it was only the beginning. Shuddering down on him, she braced her hands on his chest, took a deep breath, and got to fucking work.

"Uh! Uh! Uh!" she grunted as she bounced on his dick. He held her hips, guiding her into a galloping rhythm, accentuating each downthrust. Together, she felt his entire length with each undulation, all the way up to the head of that beautiful dick, all the way down until their pelvic bones rubbed in wet, slippery friction. "Oh, fuck! Oh, yes!"

"Yes, Chels! Fuck me! Fuck my dick!"

"It's so good!" she moaned right back. "It feels so... fucking huge!"

"Ride it. Ride it, Baby!"

She dug her nails into his shoulders, squeezed her thighs around his hips, and came in a throaty scream.

17

THE NEXT DAY

"**A**nd that was just the very beginning."

"That's so... wow, Chelsea." She'd been lightly stroking his cock as they lay there, side-by-side, but he needed more. He was going crazy. "So you liked his size?"

"I did, yes." The apologies were gone. "I liked it because it was so different."

"How many times?"

"Did I come?" she asked. "Honestly, I have no idea. I definitely lost count."

"Okay, what about Todd?"

She paused to do some mental math. "Only three times, actually. No, four. After my initial blowjob, he didn't come for a long time. He just... fucked." She giggled. "He was like a machine. A sex machine. We tried so many positions—him on top, me on top again, but facing away. Doggy. Up against the wall —maybe my favorite."

"The wall?"

"The shower wall, in that situation. That happened this morning. I woke him up with another blowjob—I gave him *so* many blowjobs." Chelsea knew exactly what to say to drive

Andy nuts. "Then we went into the shower to get ready for the day. He held me against the wall. I felt so weightless like that, no fear that he'd drop me, and he'd just bounce me on his cock, using my weight. It felt *sooo* deep, Andy."

"Did it hurt?"

"A little, but..." She nibbled on her lip.

"But amazing," he answered for her.

"Amazing, yes."

"Wait, did he bring a condom into the shower?"

Chelsea went red. "No, that was... I'm sorry. No. But he didn't come inside me. And he gets tested regularly, and was clean. And we were... we were careful..."

Andy's heart was racing. "That's so..."

"Wrong, I know," Chelsea said. "I'm sorry."

Wrong, yes. But also... "I was going to say it was so hot," Andy admitted. "Next time, as long as you know he's clean, and you're okay with it, you don't have to worry about the condoms."

Was he really saying this? They both wondered. It was now out there, though, and Andy wasn't taking it back.

"Next time?" Chelsea asked. He heard the tinge of hope in her question. She wanted more, but seemed too afraid to ask.

"It's only Thursday," Andy said. "We don't leave until Saturday, and I believe that he lives here..."

"He does." She looked furtive.

"What?"

"He kind of already... asked to see me again... if... if that's okay." Despite the wild confession, she was so adorably bashful.

"And what did you tell him?" Andy asked.

"That I needed to check with you."

She really was amazing. "You want to see him again."

"I'm..." She caught herself before she apologized again. "Yes."

"I want that, too," Andy admitted. "I want to hear more stories. I want to... maybe..."

"Watch?" She helped him out.

"If that wouldn't be too weird."

Chelsea snorted. "I've spent almost the last six months in some state of being watched, Andy. Maybe I'm becoming an exhibitionist."

"From shy librarian to sexual exhibitionist. Not something I expected," he said. "So you were in the shower, bouncing up and down on his dick..."

Her nervousness seemed to fall away, now that the subject turned back to something more graphic. Andy considered that—how much she'd changed, how it was easier to consider her physical transgressions than talk of anything more personal or emotional.

Chelsea went back jerking him, her grip growing more firm on his dick. "The shower was actually the third time that he came. After driving me wild, he pulled out of me. We made out as I jerked him off, but I knew what he really wanted. We stepped out from under the spray. I got on my knees and blew him as I soaped up my tits."

Andy was staring at her, heart racing, mind trying to catch up to all these revelations. "You... you tit-fucked him?" They'd never done that before, although Andy had always dreamed about doing it. He just never had the guts to ask.

"Todd told me earlier how he'd had a dream about doing it, so... yes. I sat up on my knees, wrapped my soapy tits around him, and let him fuck them until he came all over me."

"Holy shit, Chels. That's wild."

"So wild," she agreed. "With Todd, it was like I was this other woman. Some slut. Only... I wasn't doing it for him. I, sort of, wanted to be slutty."

"Just for him?"

She shook her head. "No, not just for him. For you. For me. For us. It's not something that I want to be all the time, but this whole thing has taught me that it can be fun to be... I don't know... like, naughty? From time-to-time?"

"Definitely." They kissed again. "My naughty hotwife."

"So you're really okay?" she asked.

"When I heard you two through the door, and heard how into the sex you were..." *God, you feel so big!* "How much you liked his big cock..." She didn't immediately apologize. Good, they were past that. "It was the most intense thing I think I've ever felt, and honestly? It hurt, but also, I cannot wait to hear that again."

"I'm sorry it hurt."

"I'm not. I think we'd have a real problem if it didn't. Or if you didn't feel as guilty as you do."

She nodded. "That's true."

"But also, you don't have to feel guilty."

"And you don't have to feel hurt. And I am going to make damned sure that doesn't happen again." She stroked him more deliberately before sinking down beneath the sheets. "I definitely need to let the kitty recover, but let me take care of this, just for starters.."

Maybe it was the long night, or the long week, or how much had changed since she'd gone off to Castaway, but it was the best blowjob he'd ever experienced. Chelsea watched him, pushing her hair from her face and fixing him with those large, dark eyes —eyes that the world had fallen in love with. Eyes that Todd had been seduced by. Eyes that were now completely wide open.

Jason may have been the official winner of Season 25 for Castaway, but Chelsea and Andy were feeling pretty good about it, too.

18

C-LIST

"I heard a rumor," Chelsea said, looking up from her phone. They were having a late breakfast in the hotel's restaurant. It was mostly empty, and they were tucked away in the back. "Kim invited you back to her room?"

So much had happened that Andy had completely forgotten about the offer. "Oh, right!" Even though he'd been good, he still felt guilty about it. "And it was actually not just Kim. She invited me to join her and *Camila!*"

It didn't shock Chelsea the way Andy had expected, which meant only one thing. "You knew they hooked up last night?" he asked.

"Where do you think I heard the rumor?" Chelsea said. "Here. No secrets." She set her phone down on the table, turned it to face him, and slid it over. "Start at the top."

There was a text thread from last night, between her and Kim.

[Kim]: So you and Todd?!?!
[Chelsea]: Yeah. Me and Todd.
[Kim]: So hot. How was it?

[Chelsea]: Amazing. Crazy. Energetic.

[Kim]: Did he have a big cock?

[Chelsea]: Kim!

[Kim]: What? You know I'm going to ask.

[Chelsea]: Yeah, it was big. And nice. And yes, he knew how to use it.

[Kim]: God, I'm so jelly! Not only do you get one well-hung stud, but your other man is such an amazing guy. You know he turned down a threesome with me and Cammy?

[Chelsea]: Wait. You invited him?

[Kim]: Sorry, hon. Couldn't resist. I was drunk and horny, and he looked ripe. Don't be mad. Like I said, he kept his honor.

[Chelsea]: And you never had any.

[Kim]: It's true. I probably would have backstabbed you in the game long before you did it to Todd. 😜 But you know I love you.

Reading the banter was fun, although Andy skimmed past it, wanting to see more scandalous content. He didn't need to go far.

[Chelsea]: So you and Camila? Really?

[Kim]: Yeah, really. I never got to tell you that on that last night, you weren't the only one getting naked. I always wanted to taste that pretty Puerto Rican, and it was pretty incredible. We even initiated Janice into the world of girl-on-girl pleasure.

Janice was the fit "mom" of the group. Reading ahead, Chelsea seemed just as shocked as Andy felt reading it.

[Chelsea]: You and Janice? No!

[Kim]: And Cammy, yes. I wanted to repeat last night, but she's got that new guy, and he didn't seem to be game.

[Chelsea]: So you came for MY man.

[Kim]: No, I CAME on Cammy's tongue. Honey, it's so amazing. You need to try it sometime.

[Chelsea]: I'm sure Andy would like that.

[Kim]: Good idea. Both of you can join me. And we can see if Todd's around, too. Make it a nice party.

[Chelsea]: You don't stop, do you?

[Kim]: Life's too short. And don't tell me this doesn't make you at least a little curious.

Andy wasn't expecting an image, let alone something so graphic. It was taken from Kim's perspective, pointed down between her open legs as Camila, the pretty producer, lapped at Kim's pussy. There was a lot to process with that photo. Kim had a little triangular brush of auburn hair above her pale pussy lips. Camila had a very long tongue that was buried between Kim's folds. Her glasses were gone, and the way she looked at the camera projected so much need.

[Kim]: Suddenly quiet over there. You're playing with yourself, aren't you?

Indeed, where all the other texts came on each other's heels, there was about two minutes between the photo arriving and Kim's followup text.

[Chelsea]: No comment.

Andy looked up at Chelsea, who glanced at her phone and saw what he was looking at. "Don't read too much into that," she said.

"Okay," he said. Even Chelsea didn't seem to believe him. "But I mean also I'm cool with you getting turned on by a little lesbian action—"

"Oh, shut up," Chelsea said with a laugh. Andy swore she was at least a little flustered. "Don't make me regret showing you that thread."

Andy pantomimed zipping his lips, only to immediately open them again to ask, "When was this?"

He answered the question himself as he scanned the time stamps. Happened in that hour earlier that morning between when she'd asked him to bring her a change of clothing and when she'd fucked Todd one more time.

In fact, the very next text was Chelsea announcing that.

[Chelsea]: Todd is coming back. Sorry, no time to answer.

[Kim]: Boo! At least return the favor with a photo of that hottie.

[Chelsea]: Stay away from my men!

[Kim]: I don't want to keep them. I just want to borrow. Now be a good friend and snap me a pic.

Amazingly, there *was* an outgoing picture. From Chelsea. Of a naked Todd. He stood proud in his nudity, and while Andy wasn't attracted to men sexually, he definitely saw why Chelsea and Kim—and so much of the internet—drooled over the guy. He was ripped, but in a real world, working man's kind of way. This wasn't a guy who got his body only from hours in the gym —although that probably had a lot to do with it. Todd was a firefighter, and his body was honed from that very physical profession.

Also, he had a giant fucking cock. Even mostly flaccid, it hung large and brown between his thighs, made even larger by the lack of pubes.

[Chelsea]: Shocker. He didn't mind.

[Kim]: Oh yummy.

[Chelsea]: Bye now!

[Kim]: Hit me back later. Enjoy that beautiful dick.

There were no more texts, but what he read was enough. Andy's heart raced. His mind reeled. Hearing Chelsea talk through her time with Todd was one thing, but actually *seeing* the man that she'd fucked made it all real. So did reading his sweet wife describing the extramarital sex as 'amazing' and another man's cock as big and nice, and how Todd knew how to use it.

"So do you want to go to Jason's thing?" Chelsea asked as she took her phone back. "I know that this must be really weird for you, not even counting the hotwife stuff."

"Which is a layer that can't really be ignored," Andy said.

"Yeah," Chelsea said.

"When I was watching you guys up on stage, it was like watching you with your family at Thanksgiving, when everyone's had a little too much to drink. You're all so close, and I wasn't a part of it."

"But you are," Chelsea said. "Because you're a part of *me*."

She was trying, and Andy appreciated that. But it also didn't matter. "You don't have to reassure me. I know you're not going to leave me for that world, just like you wouldn't leave me for your family."

Chelsea snorted in agreement at the truth of that statement.

"And I like that you've got that bond," he went on. He gestured to her phone. "I actually like that you've got that bond with *Todd*, even. You're still you, Chels. I don't think you could have done..." He felt himself starting to heat up. "I don't think you would have fucked Todd last night if you *didn't* have that kind of bond."

Chelsea looked prepared to deny it, but seemed to realize that he was right.

Andy said, "It's okay. I wouldn't want it any other way. Plus, now that I've seen what he's packing, I can't really blame you for wanting more of that."

Chelsea blushed. "Yeah, if you don't mind, I'm going to hang on to that picture into my old age."

"I don't mind, and if you want to get an action shot or two—"

"It *is* her," someone said from two tables down, interrupting their conversation.

"Told you," said another.

Turning, Andy saw that it was a couple of young women,

early twenties, their blond hair and tanned skin right at home in southern California.

"I am, like, so bummed that you didn't win," the first said.

"Uh, yeah." Chelsea didn't know how to react to her sudden C-list celebrity status. "I'm pretty bummed, too."

The other looked at Andy. "Are you the husband? Oh my God, you are!"

Andy wanted to crawl into a hole. Chelsea recovered quicker than he did. "Yes, this is my rock, right here," she said, reaching over and lacing her fingers into his. "Couldn't have made it as far without this guy."

"Aw, that's so cute! Mind if we get a selfie?" They were coming over before Chelsea could nod, and like that, Andy and Chelsea were flanked by these two, attractive blondes, memorialized on Instagram or SnapChat or whatever they were on these days.

Chelsea and Andy made a quick escape after that, heading for the elevators. "Is it always like that?" he asked, realizing that experiences like that weren't new for his wife. Like with her Pilates instructor.

"Sometimes. Most people kind of just look at me like they know me, but can't place where. Or they're not sure that I'm the Chelsea from the show."

"Is it weird?"

"Always," Chelsea laughed. "But it's not something that'll last long. The new season will start in a few months, and I'll be long forgotten."

"You're selling yourself short," Andy said. "You played a historic game."

"Oh, please. They're going to remember Jason more than me, and you know why? Because he's going to do his best to keep himself in the spotlight. He'll do the morning show rounds, maybe get a spot on Fallon or something. He'll host some watch parties and show up at events like tonight. That's how you ride this thing out. It takes work and desire for the spotlight, and that's not me."

It wasn't. The show gave Chelsea an infusion of confidence, but it didn't change who she was. She'd gone on Castaway because she loved the game, not the attention. "But we're going to the bar thing tonight, right?" Andy asked.

"I mean, who turns down free drinks?"

<hr>

ANDY AND CHELSEA spent the afternoon at The Getty, losing themselves in the art. They had lunch there under the high, blue sky, and Andy started to understand why people liked this part of the country. The weather was amazing.

A few people did a double take as they wandered the gallery, but no one else approached and asked for selfies. For the afternoon, anyway, they were just Andy and Chelsea, tourists in a new city doing touristy things.

Well, apart from when she was on the phone. Turned out that it wasn't just Jason that fans were curious about, and the network was capitalizing on it. They'd booked Chelsea on a couple podcasts, which she could do over the phone, and when they heard that she was here through Saturday, they got her some recorded spots for some of the weekend shows.

"So much for a free Friday," she said. "They've booked me throughout the day tomorrow."

"It's all good," Andy said, seeing the glow about her. "You're enjoying this, admit it."

"I don't hate it as much as I'd thought," she said. "And I do like having someone else do my hair and make up. Oh, and it's not like this stuff is unpaid. It's not a million bucks, but it's a nice bonus."

"It was never about the money."

"Yeah, I know," she said. "And this experience has already repaid itself."

"So much," Andy agreed. "Speaking of, any more 'experiences' planned for tonight."

Chelsea giggled. "We have the thing at the bar…"

"Uh huh."

Her phone buzzed, and when she read it, she grinned up at him. "Speak of the devil," she said.

"You've been texting?"

"All day," she said. "Here. For transparency."

She handed her phone back to him for one more glimpse into her world. The texts only started that morning, which kind of surprised Andy.

[Todd]: Hey. You up?

[Chelsea]: I'm literally right next to you, and I already regret sharing my number.

The next text didn't come until later, when Andy and Chelsea were getting ready to come down to breakfast.

[Todd]: Did everything go okay with your husband?

[Chelsea]: Yes, it was good.

[Todd]: And?

[Chelsea]: And he's good, so I'm good.

[Todd]: You need to reward that man.

[Chelsea]: Working on it.

[Todd]: I can't wait to see you again.

[Chelsea]: I can't wait to see your big dick inside me again.

[Chelsea]: OMG, did I really just type that? Is there an unsend on this thing?

[Todd]: I like this version of you.

[Chelsea]: So does my husband.

[Todd]: Maybe we can sneak away after making an appearance tonight.

Andy handed the phone back. He was hard as a rock. "Well that answers that."

She pressed herself close and kissed me softly. She was beyond getting worried anymore. "This time, I'm going to figure out a way for you to watch."

"I think that maybe you're becoming an exhibitionist."

19

PERKS

For the hosted happy hour even—Jason's celebratory party—Chelsea changed into her Castaway persona. She even fished out her fake, metal-framed glasses, and while it was too warm here for the buttoned-up version of the librarian, she wore a cute, white blouse and an A-line skirt with ruffles and pleats that was reminiscent enough. Her high bun helped bring the look home.

The bar that Jason had found to host them was in Santa Monica, a kitschy place down by the water called Glory Days. As the sun hovered at the horizon of the wide Pacific Ocean, it could have been a scene from Castaway. All it would take was a shot of a lonely stretch of beach and a contestant or two wander in the surf.

Turning around, Andy was presented with an entirely different picture. The bar, cast in warm, orange light, was bustling. Many of the friends and family of last night were here, crowded in, and the bartenders were busy at work. On half of the screens that lined the bar, last night's recap show was playing again, a reminder to anyone who may have wandered in that yes, this bar was hosting the Castaways.

That meant there was no hiding here. There weren't double takes or second guesses. When they saw Chelsea, they knew it was *the* Chelsea. And when they saw Andy, they saw her cuckold husband. Andy didn't love that feeling.

There was as also the matter of Brooklyn and Kyle. Last night, Andy had thought that he'd been so clever going incognito with them as they gossiped about his wife. Now he was faced with the real possibility that they'd put two and two together and call him out.

Turned out, he needn't have worried. They didn't remember him at all, and were so wrapped up in being snarky while seeming nice. When Chelsea introduced him to the showmance pairing, Brooklyn put on a fake smile and said, "It's so great to meet you, Andy." Without breaking her sunshine expression, she added, "I'd say Chelsea's spoken so much about you, but, well, you know the answer to that."

Andy felt Chelsea stiffen beside him, but was determined not to let Brooklyn get to him. "It's nice to meet you, too." He put an arm around Chelsea and looked at her warmly. "She really did have everyone fooled, didn't she? You know, when we came up with the plan together, even I wasn't sure that she'd be able to pull it off."

Brooklyn's eyes opened a little wider, and she lifted her adorably cute chin just a touch. "You... knew?"

Andy felt the cuckold yolk on his shoulders lift just a bit. "Of course."

"We're a team." Chelsea picked right up. "Andy and I talk about everything."

Rather than dispute them, Brooklyn actually turned to Kyle. "Why can't you be more like that?" she demanded.

Chelsea and Andy grinned at each other. This was how Kyle and Brooklyn had operated on the show, and Andy now knew that the bickering lovers bit wasn't an act.

Kyle said, "Like what? Like let you flirt with other guys? Baby, you know you can—"

"No, not that. Just... uh!" Brooklyn stomped off. Kyle followed.

Chelsea looked at Andy with new appreciation. "That was well done, Andy. Maybe you should go on Castaway next."

"It would be an interesting concept." Molly Reynolds surprised them. Not only was she listening to the two, but Andy hadn't expected her to attend this event at all.

"Molly!" Chelsea said, nearly jumping.

"Evening, Chelsea." Molly had a smooth and welcome demeanor. Andy immediately understood why she was such a good host. When she turned to Andy, he was also struck by how beautiful she was. "You must be Andy, the secret husband. Sorry we didn't meet last night."

"I... uhh... it's nice to meet you, Molly Reynolds."

Molly had a musical laugh. "You can just call me Molly."

"Right." Andy blushed hard. "Sorry."

"He's a cutie," she said to Chelsea.

And Molly reminded him of an anime character with her large, dark eyes and mixed ethnicity. She was a tiny thing, too, this up close, even in her platform heels. Even dressed down and casual—dark leggings, long, loose blouse, dark hair in a ponytail—she was the obvious celebrity in the room.

"And he's staring;" Chelsea said with a smirk. "You know, he's always had a crush on you?"

"Chels..." Andy said, finding some semblance of a voice, even as his face felt like it had caught fire.

Molly handled the question with grace. "Married to someone like you, Chelsea, that's quite a compliment," she said. "And if we do a spousal Castaway, maybe you'll try out. I'm sure all of America is curious to meet Chelsea's amazing husband."

"I don't..." The prospect of going to reality TV was terrifying. It was also hard to say no to this woman.

She laughed again, letting him off the hook. "It was lovely to meet you, Andy. Hopefully tonight won't be the last."

When she moved on, they both released a breath that neither realized they were holding. "I'm terrible," Chelsea said, her face red.

Andy knew exactly why she was so flushed. "Because whenever you see her, you think about her orgy?" Andy asked. "I do, too."

The evening ebbed and flowed. Andy didn't want to seem so dependent on Chelsea and gave her space to catch up with her friends—very conspicuously not including Todd. But she didn't just socialize with the other Castaways. She met her fans, of which there were many. The women last night and the blondes at breakfast weren't her only admirers. Some spoke of her savvy. Others—mostly guys—were focused on her good looks.

Andy was privy to more of those conversations, blending in with the crowd, eavesdropping as he could.

"Man, she's even hotter in person," he heard one guy say.

"For real. Talk about buxom."

"I think she looks better with a little more meat on her. Those tits, bro."

"And that ass."

They weren't all like that, and sometimes they weren't so kind to Andy.

"You buy that about how she was just friends with Todd?" This was another set of guys, along with a woman.

"Fuck no," said the guy.

"Yeah," the woman agreed. "There's just no way." She also noticed how Todd and Chelsea pointedly stayed apart. "If they were such great friends, why haven't they exchanged more than five words tonight?"

"You've been watching?" a guy asked.

"I've been watching Todd," she said with a coy grin. "I wouldn't mind if he rescued my kitty in a tree."

"Wow, really? You sound like—"

"One of you guys? Girls like sex, too. I'm sure Chelsea did on that island."

"But she's married."

The trio all laughed, clearly not believing that she was faithful at all.

Jason insinuated himself everywhere, gregarious and loud. He made impromptu speeches. He mingled with cast and fans alike, connecting people, making them feel good, doing all the things that helped him win the game.

Andy stayed on the periphery of it all, a place that he preferred. Eventually, though, he found himself in the inevitable conversation with the man who made him most anxious.

"Todd, how's it going?" Andy was determined to be the cool guy, so when he found himself at the bar, waiting on a drink next to the man who'd fucked his wife all night, he held out his hand in greeting. It didn't even shake.

"Andy, hey, man," Todd said with a welcoming grin. He took Andy's offered hand and gripped it like they were bros, even pulling him in for a hug. "It's good to meet you."

The hug felt like embracing a slab of concrete. The man wasn't all bulging muscle, but he was definitely made of muscle.

After the quick hug, Andy said, "Nice to meet you, too." He'd been thinking a lot about how to approach this meeting. He'd imagined whole conversation threads that this could take. Between those and watching the show, it felt like he knew Todd already. Throw in the beers that he'd had, and before he could stop himself, Andy was leaning in closer and adding, "Good to meet the man who's fucking my wife."

Todd recoiled, like Andy was about to hit him—not the reaction that Andy had imagined. He'd meant the statement to be more like a wink and a fist bump, not a threat.

Todd got it when he saw Andy's grin. "Shit, I thought you were about to get violent," he chuckled. "Okay, yeah. Let's go there." He raised a glass. "Thank *you*, man. Like, fuck. I am eternally in your debt."

"No debt at all," Andy said. They were closer to his imagined script once again. "You showed her a great time. Hopefully, more of the same tonight."

Todd had a chipped tooth that showed whenever he smiled. It was endearing, and he flashed it here. "I mean, I think I can free up my evening."

They got their drinks from the bar when a random person asked if she could take their picture together. Todd looked at Andy, who shrugged.

"Oh, my God, this is amazing," she said, slipping into place between the two of them as she held out her arm. She took the photo and was already loading up Instagram when she said, "So it really was an act?"

"I'm afraid it was just an act," Todd said with a sincerity that was frighteningly believable. "Although Chels and I are still pretty good friends."

"Man," the fan said. "That is so cool." To Andy, she said it again,"So fucking cool, man. Your wife is *so* my hero."

When she was gone, Andy said, "Thanks for that."

Todd waved it off. "I get it. You just need to be careful. Others..." And he said this looking toward the vicinity of Brooklyn and Kyle, "would love to drag Chels down into the dirt with them."

"Noted," Andy said. "That one seems like a real piece of work."

Todd nodded, saying, "Only person trying to cling harder to their fifteen minutes than Jason. I hear she's trying to turn it into some Instagram modeling, content creator thing. She's already organizing watch parties for the next season, which is still at least four months away."

Brooklyn wore a tiny pair of jean shorts and a tight top. She'd cut her blond hair since the Caribbean, wearing it shorter and straighter, curling in just beneath her chin.

Todd was thinking the same thing as Andy, saying, "Real smoke show, but so not worth it. I'd feel bad for Kyle if he wasn't such a prick."

"Hello, gentleman. Talking about your pricks again?"

Kim joined them, taking the place of the fan as she tried to put an arm around the two tall men. Even in her heels, the diminutive redhead couldn't quite reach, so she linked arms instead.

"Hey, Kim. You're looking good," Todd said, eyeing her. She was wearing a sexier version of what they had her wear on the show—a short, tie-dyed dress that tied behind her neck and left her back mostly bare.

She pouted at him. "I was hoping you'd wear your fireman's uniform."

"Too many people on social media already think I'm a stripper," he joked.

Her turn to eye him. "I'd hire you," she said. "But that's not why I'm here, as tempting your offer is—"

"Not an offer," Todd clarified. Kim ignored him.

"I'm done with this place. Cammy's actually house-sitting some place up in the Hills. I'm going to head up there. Want to come?"

Todd glanced at Andy, who said, "I need to check in with Chelsea."

"Oh, she's on board," Kim said. "So long as this guy," she glanced at Todd, "also goes." She leaned in and lowered her voice—although not quite low enough that Todd couldn't hear. "She knows you want to watch them fuck."

Todd stirred at that. "You know?" he asked Kim.

"Oh, sweet Todd. Always the last to know," Kim said. "Well, what do you say, Andy?"

Andy looked for Chelsea in the bar. It had gotten a lot more crowded, now that the sun had set and the Castaway promotion seemed to have shifted to a regular Thursday night. She was chatting with Jason and a couple of strangers, who seemed to be fans.

Away from the studio stylists and their persona-driven wardrobe choices, Chelsea was dressed more like herself. The maxi dress was full length and breezy on her, while still tight up top. The floral pattern and tie close shoulder straps gave it a casual, sexy, chill look.

She seemed to sense Andy looking, and when she took in the scene, she gave a thumbs up and smiled.

"I've never been up in the Hills."

20

THE HILLS

They left separately to avoid any suspicion. Kim went first. Then Chelsea and Andy, and finally Todd, each taking their own Uber.

The drive into the Hollywood Hills was long, made even longer by the heightened level of anticipation for what came next. This wasn't like yesterday, at the live show and post-party —was that really just yesterday? There was no doubt that Chelsea was going to fuck Todd, only this time, Andy would be able to watch.

There was one other important difference. "You shouldn't hold back tonight," Chelsea told him as she held his hand.

"What do you mean?" he asked dumbly, although he knew exactly what she was talking about.

"You made an impression of Camila—"

"That was mostly you and how you talked me up," I pointed out.

"She likes you," Chelsea persisted. "I may have primed her, but the rest is all you. She wouldn't have invited us up here if she didn't."

"And what does 'up here' mean to you?"

"Stop being so rhetorical," Chelsea said with a good natured laugh. "I'm saying that Camila and Kim invited you along so they could fuck you, and I'm okay with it, if you want to." She turned in towards him, running her hand between his legs. "And I'm pretty sure you want to."

"I'm... I... I love *you*, Chelsea. I don't need anyone else."

"And I love you, too, and I know you don't. I don't need anyone else, either, but last night was a lot of fun."

Hearing her confess that with such enthusiasm only made him harder. She pressed on, rubbing him through his pants. "I'm just saying that if I'm keeping myself open to new experiences, so should you, okay? We're a team, remember? And really, I don't mind. Think of it as your reward for being such an awesome husband."

NEITHER OF THEM knew what to expect as the driver wound his way up through the posh LA neighborhood. They passed mansions that must have belonged to movie stars or studio executives. There were hidden driveways where the homes were completely obscured, and ostentatious homes that made a show of wealth. The houses were perched along the steep hills, overlooking the glittering valley, and even the most modest of homes was afforded an amazing view.

The car pulled up to one of these more modest homes—a single story, mid-century modern house nestled into the hillside and surrounded by a strange mixture of oaks and palm trees.

"I could live here," Chelsea said as they strolled up to the front door. Around them, crickets chirped in the warm evening air. The stone pathway was lined with lamps. "This is nice."

"If you hadn't voted Todd off," Andy said, "maybe we could have put an offer in with your winnings."

"I doubt that," she said. "Even if taxes didn't take a chunk of the million, this place probably costs ten times that."

Andy eyed the suspicious lack of weeds, how green the grass was around the home, the way the stones around the path were raked. This home was designed to downplay wealth, and yet it was everywhere. "Yeah, you're probably right. Who's house is this, anyway?"

"Not sure," Chelsea said, stepping up to the front door. "A note."

There, taped to the wooden door, was indeed a note. *"Please let yourself in."*

Chelsea and Andy looked at one another, as if to say, *Ready to lose ourselves down the rabbit hole?* It was Chelsea who reached out and turned the knob.

The inside of the home was just as amazing as the outside—open concept, clean lines, very little clutter. The windows along the back side of the house were floor-to-ceiling panels designed to be slid open. Tonight, half of them were, letting in the warm evening air and the smells of the trees around them. Off in the distance, LA's sprawl was a blanket of fireflies.

The first thing they heard was the sound of female laughter. It floated through the space, mixing with the soft, jazzy tunes that reminded Andy of old Hollywood as depicted in the movies. Two steps in, and the laughter shifted to a moan.

Chelsea's hand found Andy's. Discovering how sweaty her palm was, he gave her a reassuring squeeze. They stepped through the front door together.

The furniture here continued the mid-century modern theme—low-backed and wooden-framed pieces that looked too sleek to be comfortable. Reclined in one of those sofas and completely naked was Camila, and between her legs was Kim, still in the tie-dyed bodycon.

"Mmm... yesss..." Camila moaned. "Right... right there..."

At the party last night, Camila was sexy yet professional in her white slacks and strapless top. Tonight, she was just sexy in nothing but her glasses.

She arched her back and cupped her tits as Kim licked her pussy. She was lean and long, with narrow hips and a pierced belly button. Her pussy was buttery brown like the rest of her body, her wet cleft devoid of any hair.

Andy squeezed Chelsea's hand tighter. She pressed close to him, rubbing his dick, but couldn't take her eyes off the girl-on-girl action. Andy could hear her shallow breathing and sensed her need in the way she stroked him.

"Want to join them?" he whispered.

Kim heard, stirring from her place on the floor. She lifted her head from between Camila's legs to look over at them. "Please," she said. "Come join us."

Camila also opened her eyes, but she wasn't staring at Chelsea. Her eyes, heavy-lidded with lust, were focused on Andy. "Yes." She pulled Kim up to her and wrapped her long, slender arms around the petite redhead. "Come join us."

The two started to kiss one another, their lips making loud, wet, smacking sounds that filled the room and fueled Andy's lust. He imagined his wife sliding into place beside the two, and it was almost too much for him to take.

Instead of joining, though, Chelsea pulled him to another sofa and started making out with him. As hot as the girl-girl show was, it was Chelsea's lust that hit Andy the hardest. Hard to believe that this was really happening. Everything around them seemed unreal—but so did every moment that preceded it.

When Andy started to unbutton Chelsea's blouse, he expected her to stop him. There were others in the room, and already things were wild. But she didn't stop him. If anything, she actually helped, urgently peeling it off before all the buttons were done. He could see her dark nipples through her pink, flowery bra. Andy couldn't resist, peeling the lacey cup down just enough to bare a hard nipple.

Chelsea gasped as he latched his lips around that nipple, feeling it tighten and grow in his mouth. She ruffled his hair, pressing her tit into his face. One strap of her bra fell from her shoulder.

"They're not going to join us," Andy heard Camila say between kisses.

"Not yet," Kim replied. "But the night is just..." Someone moaned. "...beginning."

As if in response, Chelsea started to tug at Andy's shirt. He let her pull it off, stealing a glance at the other sofa. Kim was stripping out of her little dress, flashing him a smile along with her perky, pale tits. She bit the tip of her tongue playfully before turning back to Camila.

"Watch them," his wife said. "I don't mind."

Chelsea slid down to the floor between his legs before Andy could protest—not that there was much fight in him. He quickly got over any guilt he may have felt from ogling the two women as he watched Kim wiggle her thong off her cute, little booty.

Chelsea opened his pants and fished out his dick. He glanced down at her. Her fake glasses were gone, but she still had the bun, her librarian persona in full effect, before she swallowed his dick.

Kim was back to kissing Camila, pushing her onto her back along the sofa and running her hand along the Puerto Rican's silky skin. "He's watching," Kim whispered. "Let's give him a nice show."

Chelsea started blowing him as the women rearranged themselves into a sixty-nine, with Kim sitting on Camila's face. "Fuuuuck," she sighed. Glancing at Andy, she said, "Cammy's got a nice, long tongue and... haaa... practically feels like a mini-dick."

Chelsea sucked him harder, her cheeks hollowing out. Andy groaned, wondering how long he'd be able to last before popping. Their morning reclamation sex was the only thing keeping him from coming right then and there.

Kim leaned down, completing the sixty-nine, and the two women were transported. Andy watched them go, and it was nearly impossible not to see Camila's dark hair beneath Kim's thighs and not think of Chelsea in her place.

"Uhh..." Andy groaned. He nearly came. He was right at the edge all at once, until Chelsea pressed her thumb against his prostate and stymied the orgasm. That was a new trick.

She pulled off of him, knowing exactly what he was thinking, and exactly what he wanted to hear. "Todd taught me that," she said. Her throat was raw, her voice husky. "He loved it when I sucked his dick, but loved fucking me more."

"Oh, Chels..." Andy nearly lost it anyway.

She didn't immediately go back to blowing him, sensing how close he was. Instead, she worked him with her hand as her other disappeared beneath her skirt. When Kim tossed her head and started to come, Chelsea turned to look, and Andy swore that her hands started to pick up speed.

"Uh! Uh! Uh!" Kim wasn't a quiet lover, and when she came, grinding her sex on Camila's face, she came with a wail. "Uh, fuck yeah that's good!"

Andy and Chelsea watched her as she shook out her mane of red hair, turned to them, and smiled, like a performer taking a bow. She almost vaulted off of Camila, gave her one quick, wet kiss, and crossed over to join the couple.

Andy was entranced by Kim's complete lack of modesty, his brain not quick processing what he was seeing. He wondered how someone so pale could have survived on that island under all that sun. He noted that she was a natural redhead, that her trimmed, triangular patch matched the color of her hair. Her freckles only covered her shoulders and the top of her chest, but didn't extend over her perky tits or smooth, white stomach. He wondered if he was going to fuck her.

"Hello," Kim said, getting on her knees beside Chelsea. "Mind if I help?"

As the two women locked eyes, Andy wondered if *his wife* was going to fuck her.

Chelsea glanced at Andy and nearly burst out laughing at whatever wild expression he had. "Sure, let's blow his mind."

Kim made to push her hair out of her face as she looked at Andy. "Blow something, for sure." And with that, she ran her tongue along Andy's stiff shaft.

Andy shuddered, clutching the edge of the cushions. He held his breath until he realized that he needed air, then sucked it in with halting, stuttering gasps. When Chelsea joined the redhead, licking the opposite side of his dick, her cheeks pressed to Kim's, Andy's breathing became even more ragged.

Kim swallowed him first, bobbing her head up and down his length to get used to him. Then she sucked him into her throat, staring up at him with those bright, green eyes the whole time. Chelsea just backed off, watching as she stripped out of her clothes.

When Kim pulled off of Andy and Chelsea moved in, though, Kim wasn't idle. She dipped lower, finding his balls as Chelsea blew him, and his world was consumed with soft, slippery pleasure.

When they switched again, Chelsea followed Kim's lead, bathing his balls with her tongue as both sets of eyes stared up at him, watching for when he'd explode.

Kim was caressing Chelsea's back, he noticed, and at one

point, as they were switching, she kissed Chelsea's shoulder before swallowing Andy's dick.

"Having fun now?" Camila's accented question reminded him that there was a third there. She appeared beside him on the sofa, her smile radiant. Her glasses were gone, and as much as he hated the trope, he couldn't help thinking how the change turned her from pretty nerd girl to sultry woman.

"Am I dreaming?" he asked her with a weak grin.

"I sometimes wonder that very thing myself," she said. "Could you help me out?"

"You never came."

"No," Camila said.

"You know I love to accommodate."

"My white knight," she said before climbing up him and wrapping her legs around his head. He smelled the spicy tang of her excitement, mixed with a more floral scent of soap. Her thighs were soft and warm. Her pussy flawless, and when he ran his tongue along her folds for the first time, she was so much different than Chelsea.

"Ah, yes!" Camila cried. Encouraged, Andy explored her more, tasting and teasing and tantalizing. It helped him stymie his own orgasm, but that couldn't be held at bay for long.

Camila was closer. She rode his face, clutching his hair as she veered off into her climax, smothering Andy's world. Cut off from oxygen, his senses overwhelmed, the mouths on his dick, his balls, even a finger pressed against his asshole, was too much.

As he came, his vision grew fuzzy at the edges. Popcorn lights closed in around him as he started to pass out, as his balls emptied into some wet, warm, and still sucking mouth.

"Uhhhh!" he growled, full-throated and loud once Camila released him from her thighs. "Oh... oh uhhh!"

It was Kim's mouth on his dick when he came, but Chelsea was still right there, their bodies pressed together, cheek-to-cheek. Kim swallowed his come, but a drop had escaped the corner of her mouth. Chelsea actually scooped it up with her index finger and sucked it into her mouth as the two women looked at one another.

"Thank you for sharing," Kim said.

"How about this," Chelsea said. "I'll loan him to you for the rest of the night. Just try not to return him broken."

"No promises," Kim said with a giggle. Then, she gave Chelsea a soft kiss on the lips. "But we'll make sure to show him the night of his life."

Andy, still recovering from his orgasm, was just about to ask Chelsea where she was going when she stood, and suddenly there was a grinning Todd. He was the only one with all of his clothes on, and it was almost absurdist to see him standing there in his jeans and boots and rolled-up shirt sleeves, putting an arm around a topless Chelsea who still wore her skirt, her librarian bun, and her heels.

"Have fun, you two," Kim said.

Chelsea looked at Andy with love. "I love you, honey. Give us a little time, then you can come in and watch."

Andy wanted to watch them now, but submitting to Chelsea's own desires was even hotter for him. Somehow, being denied the immediate gratification was even better.

"Have fun," he said. Then, to Todd, he grinned. "You can try and break her if you want."

Andy watched Todd lead his wife towards the bedrooms on the other side of the house. The firefighter had an arm around her, and slid that hand down the back of her skirt. Andy caught a glimpse of Chelsea's thong before the two disappeared from view.

"He really is into it," Kim said to Camila as she ran her

fingers over his revived erection. She'd crawled up onto the sofa to Andy's left.

Camila took her place opposite him, saying, "Told you." Andy felt flushed with shame before the producer looked at him and added, "It's why I'm so jealous of your wife, man. She gets a great husband with a nice dick, but also gets to play with others."

"Yeah," Kim sighed. "We should reward him for being so good."

"I couldn't agree more," Camila said.

The two leaned over, right in front of him, and started to kiss each other. This was real. He could see their lipstick, the sparkle of their makeup, the way sweat glistened at their hairline. He could smell their scents, mixing with one another, mixing with the aroma of sex.

Kim lifted her hand to the other woman's face, cupping it gently as she pushed her tongue deeper into Camila's mouth. At the same time, she stroked Andy's cock as it sprang to full and unapologetic life.

The two broke their kiss with a satisfied hum and turned their attention to Andy. Kim kissed him first, and as she did, he realized that this was the first time that he'd kissed another woman in many years—despite both receiving oral sex and giving it. It felt so good. She was soft and welcoming. The angle of their faces was different.

And then there was Camila on the other side of him, kissing his shoulder and the side of his neck. He turned to her, and she drew him in for a passionate make out session.

Kim whispered in his ear, "I wonder how long it'll take before she's riding Todd's dick?"

Andy's cock jumped at the question. Camila broke the kiss with him with reluctance, staring at him in the eyes as she addressed Kim. "Don't be cruel."

Kim tutted. "He likes it."

"I do," Andy admitted, tired of being a passenger on this ride.

Kim gestured to him, as if to say, *See?*

"You know the bedroom they went into has big, sliding glass doors that look out into the backyard?" Camila said. "And with the lights off back there, and the lights on in their room, we could probably see *everything*."

Andy didn't need to say anything. The two women were already rising, taking his hands, pulling him towards the patio outside. What a strange feeling, to be led by the hand, completely naked, by two nude women. He was a modest guy, and always had an issue with public nudity. Even now, knowing that they had a high level of privacy, it felt weird going outside, naked. He quickly got over it, though, as they skirted the pool and he caught a glimpse of what was happening in that bedroom.

"Oh, damn, they didn't waste any time," Kim said as Andy stumbled to a stop.

Todd was already inside of Chelsea. She was on her back on the end of the bed, legs open, knees up. Her skirt was gone. Her thong cast aside. Todd was between her legs, also naked, driving his big dick into her as she held him close and kissed him.

It was everything that Andy had ever dreamed of happening, all encapsulated in one moment. But this was a live situation, and the two inside were intensely alive. So were the two women with Andy.

"Pst, hey Andy," Kim whispered. She and Camila had moved ahead of him, settling onto a chaise lounge that had been laid flat. The two of them sat together, legs crossed, beckoning him to turn like sirens.

Andy didn't come to LA hoping to hook up with anyone other than his wife. He didn't need it, and she didn't 'owe' him this. But he also wasn't going to turn down this offer, and Chelsea had loaned him out.

He settled in between the two women, glancing one last find at the athletic fucking that Todd was giving his wife, then asked Kim, "So how does this work?"

She giggled softly. "We do whatever we want," she said, touching his cheek. "We do whatever feels good."

With that, Kim kissed him on the lips, and that kiss turned into something deeper and feistier. He felt something cool and wet on his dick, and for a moment he thought Kim was blowing him again. Then he realized that it was a condom.

Andy gasped and almost chickened out. This was real. This was happening. Then he looked into the bedroom, where Chelsea was getting railed by the firefighter stud, and his dick only grew more.

"You're the host," Kim said to Camila. "You get him first."

"Technically I'm just a guest," she said, "but I won't say no."

Kim moved behind Andy, pressing her tits into his back as Camila lowered herself into his lap, facing away, so that all three could enjoy the show in the bedroom.

Andy stifled his moan as he sank into Camila's tight embrace. *"Aye mi,"* she gasped. "It's been too long since I've felt... that..."

"You're her first man since they shot season 25," Kim said. "Cammy is very choosy with who she fucks."

Andy ran his hands over Camila's lean body. She had nice tits, more than a handful and perfectly proportioned to her body.

"She likes you because she loves your wife," Kim continued. "And we all love your wife."

They watched as Todd pulled out of Chelsea and stood. Andy had seen him naked before in that texted photo, but he'd been flaccid in it. Now he was erect, and he was huge. Even Kim behind him gasped at the man's impressive body.

"That's a big dick," she whispered.

Chelsea rolled over onto her hands and knees, and Todd slid up behind her, nine inches of manhood in his hand—nine inches of *unprotected* manhood. Even though Andy had told her that condoms weren't necessary, it felt like such a searing transgression. He loved it. The realization rocked him.

Todd drove into her from behind, hands on her hips, his dick ripping a cry so loud from her that they could hear it outside. "Fuck, you're so... big!"

"She must have felt that cock pressed against her when they spooned for warmth at night," Kim said, now teasing Andy. "She knew what he was packing."

He held Camila's hips and started to roll his hips to match hers—and to match Todd's. He wasn't just a watcher, and the hottie producer deserved more than a live dildo to fuck.

Camila looked back at Andy, smiling brightly before reaching back to kiss him over her shoulder.

"Play with her pussy," Kim instructed. "She likes a finger on her clit. And looks like so does your wife."

Inside, Chelsea was resting on one elbow now, her cheek to the bed, as she reached between her legs and played with her pussy. Todd started pounding her with more vigor.

Andy sought to match, doing as Kim suggested. Camila's pussy was as smooth as Chelsea's, and he heard her gasp as he found her clit. "Harder," she hissed to him as he started to play with it. "I'm not fragile. I won't... break..."

"Ahh! Ahhh!" Chelsea yelped inside. Todd was yanking her hips back into his cock, manhandling her in a way that Andy had never dared to. Chelsea seemed very into it. It was hard hitting, rabbit-paced fucking—tits bouncing, ass cheeks bouncing, hair bouncing. Todd's face was contorted as he fucked, his brow furrowed hard, his teeth clenched, his nostrils flaring.

Andy couldn't do that, couldn't match the intensity, but it was inspiring enough for him to try. He got help a moment later, feeling the wet bath of a tongue on his balls. Kim was between their legs, pushing his fingers away from Camila's clit as she used her tongue on them both.

Camila arched back into him, thrusting her chest into his groping hands as she grinded her hips into his pelvis. For a moment, his view into the room was obscured by Camila's lustrous, black hair. He gave himself to her, sweeping his hands up her body, caressing her tits and kissing her neck as her climax built and built.

Beyond her, Chelsea started to cry out a loud, "Fuck me! Fuck me!"

Andy looked inside. Todd had twisted her brown locks into his fist like a rein and was pulling her hair as he fucked her in short, urgent jabs. He slapped her ass, and she moaned even louder. "Uh, God! Uh, fuck!" Chelsea, with her head thrown back, was losing her mind. "Fuck it into me! Give me your come, Todd! Give me your... come!"

Between Andy's legs, Kim rubbed Camila's clit fast and hard as her tongue sought out Andy's taint. He'd never felt anything like it, and when she started to rim his asshole, he lost it.

Todd was there, too, up on his haunches, his body looming over Chelsea as he bore down on her, smashing his hips into her ass and driving her shoulders into the bed. He roared as he emptied his balls into Chelsea's married pussy.

"Yes! Yes, yes!" Chelsea cried. Or maybe it was Camila. Or maybe it was Andy. He wasn't sure. They were all coming. Even Kim, between their legs, had rubbed herself to an orgasm, swept up in the moment.

Andy actually flopped onto his back when it was over, unable to think straight.

But Chelsea wasn't done. She was insatiable. Covered in glistening exertion, she extracted herself from beneath Todd's body, pushed him onto his back, and dove down between his legs. He'd gone soft enough that his dick flopped around in her hand, but it didn't take her long to get him hard again.

With her lips stretched around that dick, she looked up and out towards the patio. Andy had assumed that she couldn't see them out there, watching. He was wrong. She *definitely* saw them. Her lips curled around Todd's cock, although she didn't suck off. If anything, she blew him with more vigor, wrapping her hand around the lower half of the shaft, jerking him with each bob.

With her other hand, she beckoned Andy to come closer. Incredibly, his cock started to rise. Camila pulled away, releasing him with a pleasurable shudder. "Come on," she said, taking his hand. "Let's get closer."

Kim opened the sliding door ahead of them as Chelsea finally slurped off of Todd's once-again fully erect shaft. The redhead flounced over to the bed without stopping, crawling up onto it. "May I?" she asked.

Chelsea laughed as she continued to jerk Todd. "Sure, why not."

"Imagine what we could have done as a trio," Kim said, glancing at Todd, who seemed very into the imminent double blowjob. Kim shocked both of them, though, when she reached out and kissed Chelsea on the mouth. And unlike earlier, this kiss was deep and passionate.

Andy studied his wife, the way she tensed, the way she relaxed, the way she started to kiss Kim back with equal fire.

"Is this happening?" Andy asked Camila.

The two women broke their heated kiss, turning on the cock

between them. Unlike when they'd sucked Andy off, slow and tentative, a first time partnership, Chelsea and Kim attacked their fellow Castaway's dick with lust-fueled enthusiasm. Chelsea flicked her tongue along the underside as Kim swallowed the tip. They switched, they teased, they kissed one another as they took turns on him.

"Come," Camila said, guiding Andy to the bed beside the trio. "This is what you've been waiting for, yes?"

Kim glanced up as they climbed onto the mattress, whispering something to Chelsea. Chelsea nodded, pushing Todd fully onto his back and mounted him. But she wasn't looking at him. She was looking right at Andy as Kim pointed Todd's dick at her pussy. She mouthed, *I love you,* as she sank down onto his member once again, taking that man's thickness balls deep.

This time, Kim was there to trace her fingers over Chelsea's clit. She crawled down beside them, sucking on Chelsea's bouncing tits before turning her attention to Todd. She traced a tattoo on his left pectoral, a trivialized 25. "This is new," she said. "For us?"

"Best experience of my life," Todd said. "Why not memorialize it."

"That's a great idea," Kim said before leaning down and kissing him. "Season of the Showmance." She cracked herself up with a loud laugh. She found Andy, standing beside the bed, and wiggled her ass. "My turn."

Camila produced a condom, but it was Chelsea who put it on. "Let me," his wife said, holding her hand out to him. He went to her side, right behind Kim, and tore open the wrapper. "I want to watch you fuck her while he fucks me."

Andy nodded as she rolled on the latex sleeve. Then, taking Kim's narrow hips in hand, and Chelsea positioned his dick, he felt the third pussy of the day envelope his cock.

Never in a million years did Andy think that he'd be here,

fucking one woman while his wife fucked another man beside him. Swinging and swapping weren't on his fantasy bingo card. Hell, the hotwife thing was only ever a vague idea until Castaway. Yet here he was, and it was thrilling.

He leaned over without breaking stride with Kim, so he could kiss Chelsea on the mouth. "I love you so much, baby," he said, touching her back and the nape of her neck. "I love all of this."

"So do I." Only it wasn't Chelsea who responded. The voice came from behind them, calm and amused and very familiar.

Turning, they saw her, leaning against the door jamb with her arms crossed. She wore that famously amused look on her face. Molly Reynolds said, "I fucking love it when things come full circle."

21

LOVE TRIANGLES AND THREESOMES

"Molly?" Chelsea yelped.

"Of course it's me." The Castaway host didn't seem upset. "Whose house do you think this is?"

Behind her was Camila, now wearing a robe and looking sheepish. Had they been set up? Andy started to go soft. Chelsea actually rolled off of Todd, pulling a sheet up around her. "What's going on here?" she asked.

"That's probably something I should be asking y'all, but I think I've got a pretty good idea," Molly said. "Please, don't stop on my account."

Chelsea wasn't having it. She looked past Molly, at the producer. "Did you set us up, Camila?"

"No, she didn't," Molly answered for her. "I wasn't even planning on coming out here. I leave early tomorrow for a site visit for this other project, then saw who was arriving at my house on my Ring."

"Oh, shit," Kim said, sounding more amused than not. Andy had crawled into bed beside Chelsea, but Kim actually got out of bed and was looking around the corners of the room. "Of course the host of a reality show has security cameras around her home."

"Just the front door, don't worry," Molly said. "Privacy is also very important to me." She looked at Chelsea. "And honestly, I would have stayed away except that... well, you got to see mine, so only fair that I get to see yours."

Andy was confused. Chelsea was quicker to pick up on it. "You... knew I saw you at Rescue?"

"Okay, well, maybe I gave security a short list of people who could get into that wing of the resort," Molly said. "But I was hoping that you'd join us."

"I..." Finally, even Chelsea was speechless. "I'd never. Not with BrooKyle there."

The host laughed. "And not until you were certain that your husband was okay with it, it seems. My two ex-husbands would have loved to have that kind of loyalty."

"Can someone explain to me what's going on here?" Todd said, speaking up for the first time.

"Before I... found you," Chelsea said, "at Rescue that last night, I saw Molly... in bed with... Brooklyn and Kyle—"

"And Isaiah," Molly added.

"I see," Todd said. "So that's why you looked so spooked, and were so..."

"Yeah," Chelsea said.

"You should have joined them!" he said enthusiastically. "I would have."

His brash and unapologetic horniness broke the tension in the room. Chelsea laughed, touching his chest tenderly. "I'm sure you would have."

"It's not too late," Molly said from the door, fingering the top button of her loose blouse.

Chelsea looked at Andy before responding, though. He was frozen, still pretty sure that this was a fever dream.

Camila, still cowering behind the diminutive host, said, "I'm sorry, you guys. I forgot about the door cam, and didn't think—"

Kim, who'd circumnavigated the room, stopped her with a kiss. "You can make it up to me with that long tongue of yours."

This actually got a reaction from Molly, who lifted her brows and looked at the producer. Kim noticed it, too. "You didn't know? You really should try her... if you're into girls, I mean."

"Oh, I'm very into girls," Molly said. "Just not ones who technically work for me."

"Then I'll take this temptation away from you," Kim said, lacing her fingers in Camila's. To Todd, Chelsea, and Andy still on the bed, she said, "Those three aren't off-limits."

With that, Kim led Camila away.

"I can leave you three alone," Molly said. "Plenty of rooms in this house. Unless..."

Chelsea and Andy shared one final look. When presented with the possibility of a discrete foursome with one of the hottest women on television, there was really only one answer.

Andy nodded to her, and Chelsea turned to the host. "Well, you did say that this was the best season yet..."

"Oh! Oh!" Molly barked her approval in loud and unbridled cries as Todd fucked the hell out of her. The man was unstoppable.

Andy and Chelsea were just beside them, watching as Andy slowly fucked his wife's well-used pussy. He bent low and kissed her as she wrapped her arms around his shoulders and pulled him even closer. He was exhausted. He was fucked out. But he still had enough energy to roll his hips and make slow, reconnecting love to her.

Molly was even sexier naked than she was in her fashionable clothing. She had a small, tight little body, honed from a strictly regulated diet and a small army of personal trainers. She lived in a world where image was everything, and the results showed.

"Oh, yes!" Molly practically screamed, rubbing her pussy between her legs as she backed into Todd's hips. "I'm close. Get me there. Get me there!"

Todd did as instructed. He'd been hesitant with the famous host at first, but clearly the woman loved hard sex as much as Chelsea.

That was the power of the woman. When she first came into the room, she took control immediately. Looking at the three on the bed, she told them that she wanted to just watch at first, that she'd been anticipating this moment since the live show. "My second favorite thing in the world is a good love triangle. My first?" she'd said. "When that love triangle has a threesome."

So they'd obliged. It had started tenderly, with Chelsea between her two men, kissing them back and forth as they caressed her body. Molly Reynolds slowly disrobed, distracting Andy when he wasn't kissing his wife. First, she wiggled out of her black leggings. Her long blouse went next, button by button. Her bra and panties were black and lacy, showcasing a body that had only ever been teased on television and social media.

The bra went as the threesome started to shift on the bed. Chelsea got onto her side with Todd and Andy just behind her. Opening her legs, she reached down and helped guide Todd's dick into her. Andy stole a look, wondering if he'd ever tire of watching another man slide into his wife.

Molly wasn't a silent observer. She treated the sex act on the bed like another immunity event in Castaway, offering a play-by-play.

"Watch them, Andy. Watch the way he touches her, his

hands on her thighs, that big fucking cock in your wife's tight cunt."

Chelsea didn't ignore Andy. With one man fully buried in her, she twisted so that she was facing Andy's cock, encircled it, and swallowed it whole.

"Two dicks at once," Molly continued. "Another of my favorite feelings. You can feel the way she moans on your cock, can't you, Andy? I bet you can actually feel her orgasm build as she sucks you. That orgasm's because another man's dicking your wife."

Andy shuddered. He wasn't sure how much he'd be able to withstand the raunchy commentary and even raunchier acts before him. Molly slowly approached, tugging at her thong. As Andy stared at her, she somehow became both more of a fantasy and more real at once. Her body was perfect, yet she was just a person, like the rest of them, flesh and blood—and soft, flawless skin.

She reached a hand between her legs, fingering her brazenly smooth mound. "Hold out longer, you three," she said. "I know you want to come. I know the temptation to give in is so great." She put a knee on the edge of the mattress. "But I want you to dig. Chelsea, I know you have it in you to dig, and I know that if you can wait just a little longer..." She started to crawl towards them, her tits swinging beneath her lithe body. "It'll make your release all the sweeter."

Molly crawled up to Chelsea, dipped low, and ran her tongue along Chelsea's nipple. Chelsea hesitated, slowing her blowjob, as Molly turned to look at her and ask, "Is this okay?"

Andy held his breath, watching the exchange. He didn't need to wait long. Chelsea nodded, then found her voice. "Yes. Definitely, but... I've never done this before."

"I bet you've never had two cocks before, either."

"True," Chelsea admitted.

"I've watched you do so many things that you'd never done before," Molly said, back in host-mode. "I've watched you bloom like a fucking sexy-ass flower." Well, not quite a TV-ready host-mode. "But you did it all for you." She touched Chelsea's face. "Don't stop that now. Only do this if it's what *you* want."

Molly didn't need to glance at Andy. It was unspoken. Chelsea didn't owe her husband anything anymore. She didn't need to have her first bisexual experience for him alone, and Andy quietly hoped that she knew that.

"I have the chance to pop my girl-girl cherry with the host of *Castaway*," Chelsea said, "and you think I'm going to turn that down?"

There was Molly's famous laugh, and there went the night. The guys made space between them as they watched the women explore, kissing, touching, fingering. Molly went down on Chelsea first, edging her to the brink of three orgasms without ever letting her come. Chelsea then returned the favor, and Andy couldn't believe that he was watching his wife between the legs of another woman—let alone *this* woman.

Molly summoned him up to her, and at first Andy thought she just wanted to kiss. Then he remembered what Chelsea had overheard that night at Rescue—*"Fuck my face while this slut eats me out."*

Maybe he couldn't quite do that, but when he climbed over her face and fed her his dick, she looked at him with fire in her dark eyes. Todd got into place behind Chelsea, grasping her hips and sinking his cock deep. Together, the foursome rutted on.

Still no one came. It was an unspoken endurance challenge—who could last the longest. Who would be the final one standing.

They separated into couples. Molly on her hands and knees,

getting railed by Todd. Andy and Chelsea making slower love beside them, kissing, caressing, milking the moment. They should have been the ones able to last the longest, but they also didn't have the stamina that Molly and Todd clearly had.

Chelsea looked up at Andy, her hair damp and haloed around her on the bed. She didn't say anything, but her expression said it all—*Can you believe this is happening?*

Andy could, and he couldn't. As soon as she got invited to participate on Castaway, he figured that some things would change. He figured that once the world saw past her shy librarian persona, to the vivacious woman that she'd kept private for most of her life, that would unlock something. He just didn't realize *this* was what was behind that door.

It was a door that neither of them were ready to close.

As if reading his thoughts, Chelsea clasped his hand and pulled it tight against her breasts. He could feel her heart racing. Pressing her lips to his, she murmured, "Thank you, my love. Thank you so much for coming through the front door with me." He had a momentary flash back to them coming through this very house's front door earlier this very evening, and marveled all over again at this connection with his wife.

And with that, Chelsea was the first to come, pulling Andy back into the present moment and deep into her and grabbing his ass as she rocked beneath him. It triggered his own release— and this time, he knew it would be his last of the evening. She moaned as she felt him fill her, as he kissed her neck and went slack in her arms.

"Get me there, Todd!" Molly screamed. "Give me your load!"

Todd cranked on her, thumbs digging into her cheeks, his biceps straining as he took full control of her hips. Andy knew he could never fuck a woman like that—especially not at the end of a long night of sex. He could only watch and marvel as

Todd finally gave the television host what she wanted—his come.

Molly was the last to climax, doing so only when Todd sat back, spent, and she was at the center of all of their attention. The host turned onto her back, opened her legs, and fingered herself to a screaming orgasm as everyone else watched.

Then, and only then, did everyone finally fall asleep.

22

———

THE FUTURE

"You should be on the show," Molly Reynolds said to Andy. They were in the kitchen of her home. It was the next morning. When Andy woke up, Todd and Chelsea were still asleep, but Molly was gone. He found her out here, making coffee.

"But we slept together," he said. "Oh, and thanks."

She handed him a cup of coffee before pouring one of her own. "First of all, I only sucked your cock. We didn't *actually* sleep together, other than in the literal sense," she said. "Also, I don't see that as disqualifying."

"But you and Jason..."

Molly shot him a coy smile. "What about us?"

"Not saying that anything happened—"

"Oh, things happened."

Andy stumbled for only a moment before picking back up on his sentence. "But everyone said you wouldn't do anything with him until the winner was official. Like, even at Rescue in those last days, you maintained a distance."

"Everyone thought that because that was the narrative I

wanted them to think," she said. "But I'll let you in on a secret, just between the two of us."

"And Chels. I'm not hiding anymore."

Molly considered that comment before nodding. "Sure, she's fine. You know that reward Jason won in episode 9?"

"The evening at the island spa?" He did remember it. It was the only challenge that Jason won the entire season—a personal trip to a spa, where he got a massage, a nice meal, a shower, and a real bed to spend the night in.

"Yeah," Molly said. "I was actually the real reward. And he fucked the hell out of me that night. Probably hurt his play the next day, honestly." She chuckled. "Obviously we didn't film that, and only a select few of the cast knew."

"No way."

"I can be impartial and unbiased. And I love your idea of a Castaway spouse season. It's so... delicious."

Andy was starting to realize something about the host. "Is the show just a vehicle for you to bring hot people together for you to play with?"

Molly's laugh was heartfelt and genuine. "No, of course not." She winked. "But it's definitely a perk of the position."

"Oh, fuck!" Chelsea's cry carried from the bedroom.

Molly grinned at Andy. "Looks like the love birds are up." As if in answer came a strangled howl that could only be Todd announcing his own climax.

Andy grinned back. And something Chelsea had said the night before popped into his head. "We're likely not the only ones who could use some coffee."

No secrets. They had agreed on it. So there was no reason not to head back to the bedroom where his spouse had just finished another heated round of coupling with LA's favorite firefighter.

As with nearly everything else about that oh-so-impressive house, the acoustics were amazing. Andy heard their voices long before he reached the door to the bedroom.

"I dunno, Todd," Chelsea was saying.

"Come on, Chels," Todd's tone in response straddled the line between playful and wheedling. "You know it'll be a blast."

That stopped Andy in his tracks.

"I don't think I can just blow off part of the day to 'see your place.'" Andy could practically hear the air quotes Chelsea put around "see your place."

"Besides," she continued, "the studio has me pretty heavily booked before we fly out. And we have already had several blasts together, including just now." She giggled, as if trying to soften the blow.

"Let me deal with that. I'm sure Camila can carve out some time for us. It'll be special. Just you and me. Like back on the island."

Andy's stomach lurched. He almost dropped the tray he was carrying.

"You know it was never just 'you and me' back on that island. It was you, me, a film crew, producers, the medical team. You're already buying into the illusion that they're projecting."

Todd seemed undeterred. "You know we have something. Let's chase it."

"I love Andy."

And there it was. Andy's heart started to beat again. He remembered to breathe.

"I'm not looking to mess up your marriage."

"I don't know. Kind of sounds like you are." Chelsea delivered the line with a light touch that was starting to firm up. "Andy's been at the center of everything that has gone on since the day I got cast on the show. Without him, without his support, his encouragement, his love, I never would have even tried to get on Castaway. You never would have met me. There never would have been a 'showmance'. Without his openness to this..." Chelsea paused, and Andy could just see her pointing back and forth between herself and Todd, "we never would have had all the fun. And it has been fun, right?"

"Absolutely. But what you and I have—"

"We hung out for a month," she interrupted his train before it could move too far out of the station. "An intense month, yes. Was I attracted to you? You know that I was. But it was still one month. Andy and me? It's for life."

"So this is the end?"

"Don't be so dramatic." There was a pause, and then Andy heard a loud smack. The type someone made when giving their grandmother a big kiss. Then Chelsea said, "And stop pouting. It doesn't suit you. Plus, I'm not saying that. Of course we can continue to have fun. But not alone, and not behind anyone's back."

Todd's sigh was audible.

"I just don't want any misunderstandings, and I don't want any hurt feelings. It was bad enough having to listen to Molly go on and on about a 'love triangle' becoming a 'threesome' last night. I love Andy. I'm in love with him. And that's it. That's the list. You're a lot of fun and a pretty good guy when you get out of your own way. If you're looking for more, you'll have to look elsewhere."

The kiss they shared was quieter this time, but Andy could still hear it.

"Besides," Chelsea sighed. "It's not like you're going to lack for willing applicants."

At that point Andy slipped back down the hall, and retraced his steps toward the bedroom door, taking great pains to make more noise this time. When he entered the bedroom his wife and the firefighter were busy dressing and chatting away.

"Oh thank God! Coffee!" Chelsea advanced on Andy, took his face in her hands and kissed him hard. "You are my hero!" Todd grinned and thwacked Andy on the back. Andy couldn't help but notice that Chelsea had her librarian glasses back on.

CHELSEA WAS GONE for much of their final day in LA, being zipped from studio to studio, conducting more rounds of talk shows and podcasts than she'd realized. Turned out that when cameras were on and it wasn't reality television designed to seem gritty, hair, makeup, and wardrobe ate up a chunk of time.

Andy spent the time at Molly Reynolds' Hollywood Hills home. The host was long gone, off to the airport to be flown to the next exotic location—but not before pitching him one last time on trying out for some future season of Castaway.

Kim left, too, leaving him alone with Camila. He thought that it might have been awkward, hanging out with a woman he'd had sex with just last night. It wasn't. Turned out he was pretty good with casual sex.

It was exactly the kind of day that he needed, the perfect coda on this wild week. Camila gave him space, leaving him alone in the morning, only to return with some lunch. She couldn't put her inquisitive nature in a box, though. It was what made her good on the show—her ability to connect and get people to open up.

"I've got a question," she asked as they sat out on the patio in the bright, Los Angeles sun. "When she got home, why didn't you reassure Chelsea more?"

"What do you mean?"

"Well, you basically told her to go out and play the field. You literally told her that she could be Felicity, a past player notorious for fucking other guys."

"Felicity actually fucked those other guys?" Andy said.

Camila leaned in, like even up here, in the extreme privacy of the place, there could still be ears listening, always. "Yes. We had to edit it out, of course, but she was definitely not innocent. But you're changing the subject."

"Right, I... I don't know. Chelsea told me that she couldn't tell me anything, so I didn't ask about it."

"Yeah, and that's a failing on her part, for sure. But she was nervous. She worried that she'd made this big mistake, especially when you started to act all weird—"

"I was definitely insecure," Andy said.

"Let me finish. Insecurity wasn't the problem. That's natural. It's the fact that you closed off that was the problem. She read that as disapproval." Camila sighed. "You have to understand, man, that they spend all their time on that island erecting walls and being paranoid about all kinds of shit. It's hard to deconstruct that, and when she came home and you acted so... weird..."

"It didn't help," Andy finished. "Yeah, that sucks. I see that now."

"So what are you going to do about it?" Camila's eyes blazed.

"We've already talked about it. No more secrets. No more walls. At least between us."

She nodded. "Good. I've told her to cut that shit out on her end, too." She looked thoughtful. "This stuff isn't straightforward. This fantasy—your fantasy—takes on all forms. Some need to be there, or to actually participate. Some are the opposite, excited by the total denial, or maybe excited by the sneaking around. Some like to be humiliated by the wife or her lover or both—"

"That's definitely not for me," Andy said quickly.

"So what is it for you?"

"Why do I feel like I'm being interviewed?"

Camila smiled. "It's my job. Hard to escape it, but don't worry, there are no cameras here. Only you and me."

Andy felt the intimacy between them. He didn't get into this fantasy so that he could play, too. He didn't want to be a swinger. But he also had a really good time last night with the Puerto Rican, and wondered if there would be more of that in the future.

"I guess I'm somewhere in between all that. I don't want to be denied, but I also don't mind that she could be off having fun by herself. I know that she'll be home in the end."

"You're not worried about losing her?" Camila asked gently. "They got close on the show. That bond wasn't editing."

Andy thought back to that overheard conversation, and Todd's bull-in-a-china-shop attempt to lure Chelsea into something "just for them."

"Should I be?" he asked, but it was rhetorical. Todd was never a threat. He knew that now, if he hadn't before.

"No," another voice broke in. "You shouldn't."

Startled, both Andy and Camila turned in the direction of the speaker. Smiling, framed in the door, stood his wife, dressed down in blue shorts that showcased her long legs, her comfy walking shoes, and a striped jersey that highlighted her impressive figure. Her hair was down, no trace of the librarian bun to be found. No makeup. And she still wore those pointless glasses.

"Chelsea!" Camila exclaimed, even as Andy advanced on her, enfolding her in his arms.

"Did you forget something?" He breathed, realizing for the first time how Camila's no doubt well-intentioned incessant probing had rattled him more than he realized.

"You're trembling, Baby. Looks like I got here just in time," his wife whispered.

"You're wrapped up already?" Camila was saying. "Thought you'd be out much later than this based on the schedule I saw."

"Yeah," Chelsea said breezily, leaning away from Andy to look in Camila's direction. "I did a lot of it, but at least half of it was stuff we could do via Zoom, which I can do from anywhere. So I blew it off, slipped away, changed at the hotel, and Ubered here."

"Did you check out with anyone? I mean, those events take a lot of scheduling—" Camila said. Ever the producer, even in her off minutes. She looked uncomfortable.

"Nope. Like I said, I blew it off." She gave Andy a sly, sidelong glance. "It was Todd's idea."

"You're meeting up with Todd?" Camila said.

"Not till later. He wants to show us his place." Did she place a particular emphasis on "us," or was Andy hearing things?

"Right now," Chelsea went on, "I'm here to claim my wonderful husband back from you and take him to the Getty over in Malibu, then Musso & Frank's for dinner."

"But Chelsea," Camila said slowly, deliberately. "You have contractual obligations. You can't just—"

"Oh come on, Camila." If anything her smile got wider. "It's over. The show is over. And I'd say the studio and the producers have more than gotten their investment back where I'm concerned." And then she mouthed the word "showmance" with a flourish that made Andy chuckle.

"I personally don't disagree," Camila said hastily, and for the second time in their brief acquaintance, Andy saw the sexy producer seem actually flustered. "I just don't want to see you get in any trouble."

Chelsea sighed, pulled back from Andy, and advanced on Camila, giving her a big hug as well. "I know you're looking out for me. And I'm grateful. But I'm not BrooKyle, and I'm certainly not Jason. I'm really grateful to the show, too, for the experiences, every last one of them. But would I really be the person you seem to think I am if I just continued on with this....you know....this *role*?"

Camila took Chelsea by the shoulders and held the taller woman at arm's length, peering at her through her heavy framed glasses. "No," she finally said. "No, I don't think you would."

Chelsea beamed, leaning in to kiss the other woman's cheek. Then she turned and grabbed Andy's hand in hers. "Uber's waiting."

But before they had gone three steps, she stopped, turned back to Camila, reached up and removed the glasses. Folding them carefully, she held them out to the producer.

"I almost forgot," she said. "I won't be needing these anymore."

Camila's smile in return was practIcally conspiratorial. "No," she said, eyeing Andy meaningfully. "No, I can see that you definitely won't."

"DON'T WORRY," Chelsea said to Andy as their Uber driver pointed her Toyota Corolla westward toward Malibu. "Katerina doesn't speak much English. We're communicating with text messages."

Upon hearing her name the driver smiled at them both in the rear view mirror, then returned her attention to the traffic on I-10.

"You really did blow everything off?" Andy asked.

"Not *everything*," Chelsea said. "And Todd *did* invite us over for later." She ran her fingertips along her husband's thigh as she said it. Andy felt himself begin to once again harden.

"'Us,' huh?" Andy asked, his tone skeptical.

"I *knew* it! You *did* hear us!" Chelsea began to tickle the inside of his knee. "No secrets, Andy!"

He tickled her ribs in self-defense, and then a look in the mirror from Katerina caused them both to stop, smirks in place, attempting to hold back the giggles.

"What about all of those other appearances?" Andy said once he had caught his breath.

"Remember what Molly said? 'Only do this if it's what *you* want.' And she was right. And not just about trying girl-girl sex."

"At which you slayed," Andy smiled at her.

"I *did* slay!" Chelsea agreed. But she was still her, she also flushed bright red as she said it. "Anyway, I was sitting there telling the thirtieth podcaster what an 'amazing' experience the show was, and that yes, I really *am* married and yes, really, *really* happily, and *no*, there wasn't *that* sort of chemistry with Todd, and I just thought, 'I have done my bit. I don't want to do any more of this.' And from there, it's a pretty short trip to, 'I'm here for one more day with my best friend and husband.' What I *want* is to go see all of the statues the Gettys brought back from Europe with you, Andy."

"Not Todd?" he teased.

"We're talking about the same guy here, right? Can you imagine Todd among all those buck naked statues? 'My pecs are better than his, don't you think?'" She did a decent impression of the hunky fireman's voice.

I laughed. "Okay, that's fair."

"But you know that's not the reason I want to spend the afternoon with *you*, right?"

"I know." Andy leaned in and gave her a deep, powerful kiss. "I *know.*"

"Like I keep saying in all of those interviews, we *are* a team!"

Sunning themselves in the courtyard of the Getty's modern take on a Roman villa, Andy said, "You know, I didn't think you could do much to top the view from Molly's patio, but this..." His gesture took in Chelsea, but not the hills beyond her. "Perfection."

She leaned close and rubbed the tip of her nose against his. "Flattery will get you *into* my pants, you know."

"I think Todd's been rubbing off on you," Andy said.

"Ditto?" The two laughed, clutching one another in a close embrace.

"Speaking of, you *were* planning to tell me all about how Todd tried to lure you away for some stolen moments at his bachelor pad, right, 'Miss No Secrets'?"

"Honestly, I couldn't wait to tell you. It was so hilariously ham-fisted, so Hollywood." Her eyes brightened. "So reality TV. If I didn't know better, I'd think the showrunners scripted that."

Andy went cold. "You don't think..."

"No..." Chelsea said, although she seemed to be clearly considering it. "No, I don't... no. They wouldn't do that. I'm really not going to miss this life under a microscope."

"No? An introverted librarian like you, not wanting the spotlight?" He brushed her hair from her face. "A small part of you will. I know it."

"Maybe later. Right now, if I have to tell one more 'influencer' how grateful I am to the show for the 'hardest challenge' of my life any time during the next *year* or so, I think I might just *snap.*"

This was Chelsea at her core, overwhelmed by social obligations and a packed schedule. But also, she was changed, different. Andy got the feeling that she really would miss the whirl and glitz and carefully scripted pageantry of a TV show like the Castaway season finale. She would never admit it, though.

"Besides, while the show was in part responsible for the

'hardest challenge' of my life, that challenge had nothing to do with immunity challenges and making and breaking alliances."

"It wasn't?"

"No. Coming home and telling you that I nearly fucked away the best thing I've ever had. Deciding to tell you and be ready to commit to whatever penance saving our marriage required. *That* has been the 'hardest challenge' of my life."

"You were never in any danger with me."

"I know that now. And I'm so grateful." She made a face. "I've been using that word all day. 'Grateful to the show,' 'grateful for the experience.' What I feel for you is so beyond that. I have to come up with a better word."

"You librarians, always trying to categorize and name things."

She laughed. "Semantics are important, dear."

"How about just focusing on the thing where we're good," Andy offered.

"We *are* good. But that takes work and trust and talk. And now that I know what it feels like to watch the love of my life in the arms of someone else, I understand that it doesn't come easy."

Andy gulped. "I thought... you said..."

Chelsea was so perceptive. It's why she did so well on the show. Andy couldn't hide anything from her. But she didn't hold it against him, either. She was gentle as she explained it to him. "I know you were quiet about the parts that bugged you, but we can't have that sort of relationship, honey."

"You said you were okay with it," Andy managed to get out this time.

"I was, and I am. But it's fresh in my head and I still feel mixed about it. It both gets me going and fills me with terror. I want to share that with you, too."

"Same." Thinking about the show, Andy grinned and added, "We can be an alliance."

"Oh, God. Now you're trolling me. How about: 'We're a team'? If we're going to do this swinging thing, then I want you there, holding my hand while I come with someone else, or you do. I want us doing this together."

"Swinging." Andy gulped. "That's what we're doing now?"

"If you want to."

"I want to try," Andy said, his voice so small.

"I don't want to have to worry about what I told you, and think, 'Did I forget anything?' Besides... I really liked it when you were watching."

"And less hot when I was distracted?"

"Makes me sound like Brooklyn—"

"You could *never* sound like Brooklyn."

She kissed him, putting the world into that kiss.

"This is another part of why I want you with me. Castaway was great for my confidence, but you are too precious to me to leave out of any aspect of this sort of fun." She took a deep breath. "Which is why I say screw the phone and vid and texted pics. I want you *with* me at Todd's tonight."

Andy cocked his head and looked at her. "How will Todd feel about that?"

"He'll get over it very quickly. I'm pretty confident about that. Away from the island, surrounded by his life here in LA—his whole 'Come *ON*, you *know* you think I'm gorgeous' schtick—is a reminder why I don't usually go for guys like him."

"Seemed like you went for him last night."

Chelsea only flushed a little. That was a huge change for her. "I mean, Todd has a great cock and abs for days and he knows how to use both. But come on, honey. *You* light my fire in ways you aren't even aware of."

"Wow," Andy said.

They kissed. Both coming together at the same time. A lover's kiss. A sweet kiss. A soul kiss. "So what do you say, Andy? Want to come hold my hand as I give Todd a farewell fuck?"

"Well, we *are* a team."

Chelsea hugged him tightly. "And I want you *there*. I need you there. If seeing you watching tonight is half as hot as it was at Molly's the other night, we might just burn down Todd's swell little place by the beach!"

23

CLOSURE

Chelsea gave Andy one last kiss before pulling back. Her hair had fallen around her face, and when she pushed it over her ears, he was reminded of the shy librarian he'd first met.

But she was naked now—they both were—and they were in another man's bedroom. She squeezed Andy's thighs and mouthed, *Enjoy.*

Behind her, Todd was reclined in the bed, holding his nine-inch erection. His grin was wide and eager. As Chelsea had said, Todd's consternation lasted only up to his first kiss with Chelsea. He knew the score. He got it, and he seemed at peace with it.

Andy watched Chelsea's naked body from behind—tall, curvy, so sexy. He watched as she straddled Todd's prone body, squatting over him and reaching between her legs. He could just see her fingers slither along her smooth lips as Todd pointed his dick at her pussy. When she felt his cockhead against her, she moved her fingers from her mound to him, encircling his shaft, holding it steady as she slowly lowered onto him.

"Oh, yes…" she sighed as her pussy stretched around all of that girth. "Oh, oh, ohhhh yesss."

She savored the sensation, getting used to his size until she was sitting fully on the tops of his legs and that dick was buried to his shaved balls. She was leaning over him, presenting only her ass, a bit of back, a hint of her shoulders. Todd rested his hands on her haunches and flexed his hips up into her as she started to ride him.

Andy had been resisting playing with himself, not wanting to blow too soon, but he couldn't any longer. Not with that angle, not with the perfect view of Todd's dick sliding in and out of his wife. Andy wrapped his fingers around his steel-hard cock and slowly pumped as he listened to Chelsea's moans and gasps.

As hot as that was, it was even more searing when she leaned over and tried to kiss him. The wet smacking sounds broke the groans and soft cries, infusing the graphic sex with tender moments. They may not have feelings for one another, but they certainly had a physical connection. Andy had to take his hand off of himself, fearing he'd pop.

CHELSEA LIFTED off of Todd until that specimen of a dick slipped free. She grabbed the shaft and rubbed it up against her clit before reinserting, saying, "Remember when we did this back at Rescue? Remember when I felt this dick against me for the first time?"

"I'll never forget it," Todd said. "I dreamed about it for months after."

Chelsea glanced over her shoulder, meeting Andy's eyes. This conversation, this scene, was all for him—to get him caught up, to bring him into what she had with Todd. "This is how close we got," she said, rubbing her smooth and slippery lips along Todd's shaft. "We were humping like this. We were kissing..." She kissed Todd. "Like this."

And she raised up, rubbed her clit with the crown of his

dick, and pressed just the tip inside. "And then he pushed into me." She gasped. "Just... this... much..."

Todd reached up, grabbed her ass, and pulled her down to him. "And now you won't say no to anything."

They went back to fucking, athletic and intense. Todd's hands were tattooed, Andy noted as the other man grabbed her ass, squeezed, driving her down harder. His hands were all over her, rubbing up her back, driving his nails along her shoulder blades, pressing a finger against her asshole.

She lifted her head, tossing her hair. Andy couldn't see it, but knew that the man was sucking her tits, maybe even nipping at them. She cried out before pressing her hips against him, grinding there, coming hard.

Todd directed her off his lap. She knelt to the left of him, wrapping a hand around his shaft before taking him into her mouth. Todd pulled her damp hair out of her face so that Andy wouldn't miss a thing—not the way she rubbed her spit and girl-come into his balls, or the way she bathed his dick with her tongue, or how into the blowjob she was.

Todd played with her pussy as she did it, his wrist and fingers rubbing her in time with her plunging head.

"Fuck, babe, that feels so good," Todd groaned. "Now show your husband how much dick you can swallow."

Chelsea's eyes had remained on Andy, as much as she could during a blowjob. He could see her smile in her eyes now. Then she swallowed two thirds of his dick without hesitation, paused to get acclimated to the size, then slowly choked on even more.

When she'd taken most of it, she paused a moment, letting him savor the deepthroat, then pulled off and sputtered for oxygen. Then she did it again, and again, and again, each time taking more until she was able to touch her lips to the bare skin of his pelvis.

"You're a quick learner," Todd said. "But then again, you proved that with how well you mastered Castaway."

Chelsea gave him one last, wet suck before straightening up again. This time, when she lifted her leg over his body, she faced reverse cowboy so she could look directly at Andy. She planted her feet on either side of dTodd and braced her body behind her on her arms, so she was leaning back.

There was her bald mound, and there was Todd, holding his dick against her flowering folds. He slipped into her without resistance. Andy loved watching her facial expressions, the way she bit her lip and tightened her brow, the way her mouth hung slack as Todd started to thrust up into her.

She tipped her head back, her throat muscles shifting and flexing as she moaned to the ceiling. Her tits bounced as they fucked, his strange, tattooed fingers holding her by the hips, his splayed legs keeping her own legs spread for him.

He pulled out of her at one point, his dick pointing straight up as she rubbed her bare pussy along it like a dildo. Neither of them used their hands. All the play was in the hips, in the way Chelsea gyrated her lips like a stripper, buffing his phallus with her smooth, soft folds.

And then he was back inside of her, fucking up into her with loud slapping thrusts—their final stretch. Still keeping one arm back, she reached down and started to play with her clit as she drove harder into him, faster, as her cries grew more desperate. He grabbed her tits, playing with her nipples, squeezing them, pinching them.

"Yeaaasss!" Chelsea cried. He was fucking her like a jack rabbit, thrusting so hard that her cries skipped and modulated like a radio losing signal. "Uhh—yes! Yes! I'm fuckin—I'm cuuu —MING!"

She pressed down on her clit hard as she hit her ceiling.

Todd fucked her through her orgasm, but didn't come himself. Not yet. The man was a stallion.

Opening her eyes, she found Andy across the room, and crooked a finger in his direction. "I know you enjoy watching. Come closer. The view is better."

She was right. He climbed up onto the bed, close enough to hold her hand, close enough to kiss her and play with her tits as she began to ride him again. He could see everything—not like television or video, not through the filter of a lens or clever angles.

He was right there with her, listening to her breath catch and her skin slide across Todd's. He could smell her sweat and Todd's musk, mixed with the familiar scent of her shampoo. And he could see the way she enjoyed herself, the sheer physicality of the moment.

Todd was there, too, sprinting across the finish line. Andy watched and knew that this was it, this was the end. This, at last, was closure between these two. He watched as Todd's balls lifted, how the muscles of the other man's thighs rippled. How, after thrusting up into Chelsea one last time and burying himself deep in her snatch, his milky come oozed out around his shaft, drooling over his hairless balls.

Chelsea screamed as she felt it. She reached out, grabbed Andy, and pulled him in for a torrid, sloppy, glorious kiss. "Thank you," she breathed. "Thank you, thank you, thank you."

The night was far from over. They went late into the night— and by they, Andy meant Chelsea and Todd. Turned out, closure took until 3 in the morning and a lot of glasses of water. Still, Andy would be left with so many vivid memories of things that he never thought he'd even wanted.

"You're so wet."

"And you're soOHHH... big! Ahh!"

The sounds of fucking, intense and unintelligible and

undoubtedly authentic. She made noises that Andy had never heard from her and he'd certainly never fucked her with the same skin-slapping intensity that Todd gave her.

"Fuck, you're so hot, Chels. I want to do nasty things to your body."

"Then do it."

Spank!

"Ah!"

"You like it rough."

"Sometimes!"

"Naughty!"

Spank!

"You naughty, dirty librarian!"

"Ah! Yes! Spank me!"

Slap!

"Punish me! Mmm! Pull my hair!

Was this real?

Was any of it real?

Other flashes came, moments that Andy knew were solidifying into memory.

An image of the two of them standing in the kitchen, naked, sharing a beer.

A thought of Andy fucking her from behind as she sucked Todd back to life.

And a final one—Andy and Todd shaking hands, saying goodbye. *No hard feelings, and thanks for showing my wife a good time.*

"That was crazy," Chelsea said as they stepped out into LA's early morning.

Andy squeezed her hand. "And I can't wait to do it again."

24

EPILOGUE

In Todd's final interview, taken from Rescue the morning after he'd been eliminated, Todd had cleaned up. He wore a baby blue linen shirt with too many buttons undone. He'd shaved.

The video began with him just sitting there, smiling at the camera, rubbing his smooth face like he was still getting used to that sensation. With a final chuckle, he started in. *"What can I say? She got me."* He shook his head, his eyes drifting to something off-camera as he quietly repeated, *"Yeah, she got me."*

The video cut forward. *"I get why she did it. It was strategic, and Chels was always way more strategic than me. I just tried to kick ass in those challenges, do my part around the camp, and not totally piss people off."*

"I think I played a f<bleep>ing great game, though. Sorry, sorry, no swearing. Yeah, I'm proud of the game I played. Don't think I could've done it any different."

"Yeah, well, I'm still a little pissed off at her, sure, but whatever. It is what it is, you know, and I wish her the best. She could win if those f—I mean, those freakin' jackals don't take her out. She's sure as hell got my vote, and that's not because I've got a crush on her."

The producer asked him something that couldn't be understood.

"Yeah, I'm crushing. She's the f<bleep>ing real deal. Chick like that doesn't look twice at a guy like me in most situations, you know? She's a librarian for Chrissakes. But that goes for everyone who played. We're from all walks. It's what I love about watching it, and I'm grateful that I got to be a part of it."

He gave that last smile before ending the video.

"And who knows, maybe we'll see how things shake out after the show between us. If I can forgive her, I mean." He winked. By this point, he'd already forgiven her.

Andy watched this video often in the weeks and months after Castaway, as if he needed a reminder that any of this had actually happened. It's amazing how time can erase even the most intense of emotions.

He always followed up Todd's exit interview with Chelsea's final, interviewed words.

"So close. So close!" She was laughing, shaking her head as she looked up into the bright, blue sky. Like Todd, she looked reborn from the ragged woman on the beach. A shower, a good meal, and a full night of sleep in a real bed would do that. They'd put her into a sundress and clipped her dark hair back behind her ears. She sighed.

"What's one regret? Casting Todd away. That was a really hard decision. I didn't sleep at all the night before, or after. Probably why I blew that final challenge. You know, if you'd told me on that first day that the hot firefighter with all the tats would be my closest ally, I would have laughed. When he was gone, though, I felt completely... lost..."

She gathered herself. *"But you know what? In the end, I needed to play my own game. I told myself that if I made it to the end, I'd stand on my own."*

"I came into this game thinking that I wouldn't last more than a

few days. I didn't think anyone would take me seriously. They'd see the nerdy, awkward girl. But by the end..." She sighed. "Ah, the end... By the end, they saw me as a big threat and that's just crazy! Me, a threat in Castaway! Right? This game changes everyone. I've learned so much about myself out here. I've grown so much, and you know what? I know that I'm still growing. We're always growing." She snorted and started laughing. *"God, that sounds so corny. Please cut that."*

Chelsea was right, she had changed, yet she was still her amazing self. She was just much more confident with who she was now.

"Castaway has been a gift. Seriously, honestly. It's been one of the hardest things that I've ever done in my life, and I love it for that. But..." She smiled. "At the same time, I cannot wait to be home. Soon, so soon, I'll be... home."

"What are you watching?" Chelsea asked, seeing Andy on his phone. She came over, wrapped her arms around him from behind, and nodded. "That again?"

"I don't think that I can do this," he said, switching the phone off.

"Too late now," she said. "The studio car's on the way now."

"There are alternates."

"I'm not you. I'm not as strong as you." He turned in her arms, glancing behind her at the bed, where *their* bags were packed.

"Well, you're in luck then, because this time, we'll be together."

The doorbell rang. Their ride was there.

"So *The Grand Journey*, huh?"

"Think of it as a free trip around the world," Chelsea said. "Like a vacation."

"With millions of viewers watching, challenges and puzzles, and let's not forget a bunch of other teams out to get us."

Chelsea nodded. "Yup. Like I said, a vacation."

"*Castaway* really has changed you."

The doorbell rang again. "Come on. Time for our next big adventure."

ABOUT KENNY WRIGHT

Kenny has been publishing hotwife erotica for over ten years (and writing for much longer than that). He writes what he likes to read: steamy, explicit erotica that's just crazy enough to be true. He believes in a world where men read and appreciate erotica, and hope to contribute to it word by word.

Find him online at www.kennywriter.com, on Patreon as KennyWriter, or follow him on Twitter at @kennywriter and Medium.

ALSO BY KENNY WRIGHT

Like what you just read? Check out these other books by Kenny Wright (or browse my catalog at http://www.kennywriter.com/books/).

Everyone's a Winner

Who says a couple can't have new adventures after two decades of marriage?

When Lauren heads to Las Vegas alone, Eric encourages her to explore their hotwife fantasies. What ends up happening is a series of experiences that cross lines that Lauren never thought she would, and leave Eric wondering who he married and how he got so lucky.

Follow Lauren and Eric's journey, and find out just how everyone wins.

Find Everyone's a Winner online.

The Blonde in 3C

From neighbor to friend to wife to... hotwife?

Cooper always had a crush on Annika, the blonde in apartment 3C. She was friendly. She was pretty. Best of all, she had loud sex with her boyfriend, Brett, that Cooper could hear through the floorboards. He never thought that one day, he would marry that sexy blonde.

But first impressions are hard to shake, and Cooper's first impression of his future bride was of an insatiable woman he could never fully satisfy. He was always waiting for the other shoe to drop, for a new man to take his place, for him to lose it all. A hotwife fantasy was born and it grew with their marriage.

The things that Annika did for love always surprised her, but that was just who she was. She gave all of her energy to a relationship. She'd done some wild things for her hedonistic former boyfriend, Brett. She was still trying to figure out Cooper.

When they attend Brett's wedding, Annika and Cooper are put to the test. Will Annika be tempted by the past? Will Cooper's repressed fantasy explode into the open?

Find The Blonde in 3C online!

Bull's Eye Series (5 books)

Paul Sharpe, self-avowed bachelor, works hard and plays harder—always looking for a new conquest. Blondes, brunettes, redheads, he enjoys them all as long as the pursuit is fun and they're up for a good time. He's fine being disposable. Life is simpler that way.

Until he meets a woman who opens his eyes to a whole new world—the world of hotwives and cuckolds and the games that they play. After that, he sees it everywhere. At bars, at clubs, at his company's gala, he sees men furtively watching other men hit on their wives.

Can he be the other man? Can he be the bull?

Follow Paul's epic journey over five books as he evolves from the bull to so much more.

Bull's Eye 1: Discovering the Hotwife Fantasy

Bull's Eye 2: Exploring the Hotwife Fantasy

Bull's Eye 3: Enjoying the Hotwife Fantasy

Bull's Eye 4: Consequences of a Hotwife Fantasy

Bull's Eye 5: Beyond the Hotwife Fantasy